PRAISE FOR
ZORA and ME: THE CURSED GROUND

"Goose bumps, tears, smiles, and sighs: these were the rewards I took away from this exquisite read. I feel confident that my aunt Zora, the 'Zora of the Cosmos,' is quite delighted with the literary enchantment of T. R. Simon." —Lucy Hurston, niece of Zora Neale Hurston and author of *Speak, So You Can Speak Again: The Life of Zora Neale Hurston*

"A stunning work of imagination and a deeply necessary read." —Michael Eric Dyson, *New York Times* best-selling author of *Tears We Cannot Stop: A Sermon to White America*

"The connection between slave times and Zora and Carrie's world unravels slowly and with well-crafted suspense and a horrifying surprise twist." —*The New York Times Book Review*

★ "T. R. Simon's writing does elegant justice to the grown-up Hurston's genius as a writer as well as to the character she apparently was as a child." —*Shelf Awareness* (starred review)

★ "Truly profound, timely, and important." —*The Horn Book* (starred review)

★ "Simon offers keen insight into how the past affects the present, no matter how many years between them." —*School Library Journal* (starred review)

★ "Powerful, unflinching storytelling, worthy to bear the name of a writer Alice Walker called a 'genius' of African-American literature." —*Kirkus Reviews* (starred review)

ZORA AND ME

THE CURSED GROUND

T. R. SIMON

CANDLEWICK PRESS

For Richard Jonathan Simon and Viviana Mireille Simon

Copyright © 2018 by T. R. Simon

Epigraph from *Their Eyes Were Watching God* by Zora Neale Hurston.
Copyright © 1937 by Zora Neale Hurston.
Renewed © 1965 by John C. Hurston and Joel Hurston.
Reprinted by permission of HarperCollins Publishers.

First paperback edition 2020

Library of Congress Catalog Card Number 2018958248
ISBN 978-0-7636-4301-0 (hardcover)
ISBN 978-1-5362-0888-7 (paperback)

20 21 22 23 24 25 TRC 10 9 8 7 6 5 4 3 2 1

Printed in Eagan, MN, U.S.A.

This book was typeset in Centaur MT.

Candlewick Press
99 Dover Street
Somerville, Massachusetts 02144

visit us at www.candlewick.com

There are years that ask questions and years that answer.
Zora Neale Hurston

PROLOGUE

There are two kinds of memory. One is the ordinary kind, rooted in things that happened, people you knew, and places you went. I remember my father this way: laughing, picking me up, singing lullabies in his gentle bass. I see him swinging my mother in a half circle, the hem of her blue skirt flying up to show the rough white thread she used for mending, like a bed of stars along a ridge.

The second kind of memory is rooted in the things you live with, the land you live on, the history of where you belong. You tend not to notice it, much less think about it, but it seeps into you, grows its long roots down into the richest soil of your living mind. Because most of us pay this second kind of memory no mind, the people who do talk about it seem to us superstitious or even crazy. But they aren't. The power of that memory is equal to any of the memories we make ourselves, because it represents our collective being, the soul of a place.

After losing my father, after nursing myself to sleep nights on end with glimpses of the past with him, I was well enough acquainted with the first kind of memory. But by twelve I was still too young to pay much mind to the memories held by the town we lived in, by Eatonville itself.

That all changed the night we found Mr. Polk, his blood soaking into the earth. When I look back, I wonder how it had never before occurred to me that Eatonville, America's first incorporated colored town, might have a history that stretched back beyond its name and my twelve years. How could I have thought our town began with Teddy, Zora, and me, that it had just opened into the infinite present of our young lives? In fact, we were living out Eatonville's history as blindly as pawns in a century-old chess game. We were no more new or free than the land itself, but like all young people, we confused our youth with beginning and our experience with knowledge. It wasn't until that night—when we heard the town mute speak to the town conjure woman—that Zora and I began to forge a real connection with the land, a connection that let us know ourselves through a past we hadn't lived but was inside us all the same.

EATONVILLE

1903

CHAPTER ONE

———◦—◦———

I lay wide-awake in the dark, watching the flares of faraway lightning light up the hand-hewn beams of my best friend's bedroom. It was well past midnight. Light rain drummed gently on the tin roof, nervous fingers anticipating the storm that hadn't quite reached us yet. Zora was next to me in the narrow bed, deep asleep.

I was staying with Zora's family for the week while my mama tended her employer's sick baby over in Lake Maitland. After Daddy died, there was just me and Mama. I was an only child. Alone with Mama I might have felt lonely in the world, but I had Zora, my best friend, my secret keeper, and my talisman against sorrow. From the time I was old enough to have a conversation, Mama always liked to tell how my three-year-old self toddled over to Zora, who was squirming and fussing one pew away from us in her father's church, grabbed her hand, and didn't let go for the next hour. Zora took a long look at me, tried once to shake me loose, then settled right down to the idea of us being joined. Zora's mother liked to say that after I took a hold of Zora, Sunday morning service once again became a place of worship and peace for her. I don't remember that at all. In fact, my own first memory of Zora has the roles reversed: instead of me grabbing her, she's grabbing me and pulling me with her as she scrambles after a lizard that turns out to be a baby diamondback rattler. My screams brought our parents running, and Zora was praised for saving me. Only, I knew there would have been no need to save me if she hadn't taken hold of me in the first place. But I never held the scrapes against Zora. She made life in a town no bigger than a teacup feel like it held the whole world.

Thunder cracked softly in the distance. I had just closed my eyes when the shrieking began. It came from right outside—high-pitched and truncated. A shiver ran through me before I recognized the sound: horses!

I slipped out of bed and went to the window. Two horses were in the yard below. One whinnied again and they both galloped away, jumping the low garden fence almost abreast.

A hand touched my back and I jumped.

"Shh," whispered Zora. She was just behind me, staring after the retreating horses.

Still spooked, I gave her arm a squeeze. "You about scared me out of my skin!" Zora held a finger to her lips and pointed to her older sister, Sarah, and her little brother, Everett, who shared the bedroom with her. She took my hand and pulled me out of the room.

"Those are Mr. Polk's horses. How you reckon they got loose?" she whispered.

"Something scared them."

We crept down the stairs, careful to avoid the tattletale creaking spots. Zora motioned for me to keep following her. At the front door she cloaked her nightgown with her brother John's work jacket and handed me her father's work shirt.

"Something's wrong if those horses are loose.

Maybe we should go see." Her worried whisper didn't match the glint of excitement in her eye—the one that spelled adventure and trouble all at the same time.

I hesitated. Zora's plans often led me to do things that went against my inclination, not to mention my better judgment. Tonight had *trouble* written all over it, and nothing in me ever caught a thrill from courting trouble.

"Wait," I said. "Let's wake your daddy. He'll know what to do."

Zora shot me a scathing look. "Daddy will tell us to go back to bed." I sank back on my heels and crossed my arms. Zora shook her head. She knew my posture meant that I was closed for business.

"Carrie, you sitting at the feast of knowledge, but you don't want to eat. Now, I want to pull up a chair and have a heaping plate—only I don't like to eat alone. Come on, don't make me go over to Mr. Polk's by myself."

Her sorrowful pleading was weakening my resolve, but I still shook my head.

Unfortunately, Zora had caught the split second of my ambivalence and used it as a shortcut across the field of my will to the junction of our compromise.

"OK, let's make a deal. If there's any trouble, we'll

get help." She hooked her arm through mine, but I didn't budge.

"Promise?"

"Promise! I promise! Now, come *on*."

Oh, how I wished Zora couldn't lasso me so easily with her words! But before I could add another condition to her promise, she was opening the front door and yanking me through.

The night was surprisingly cool for late June. The storm clouds hovered over Eatonville but didn't break, sending down a bleak drizzle instead. Not even the moon had gumption enough to peek out from behind the thick curtain of indigo clouds as we carefully picked our way through the dark.

I followed Zora, as close as her own shadow.

"Scaredy-cat," Zora mocked. From behind her back, I could feel her smiling.

"Am not. And don't laugh at me."

Zora snorted. "Are too."

"Am—OK, you know what? Not everybody thinks trouble is an invitation. Some of us think it's a skull and crossbones sign, saying, *Keep away if you don't want to get hurt.* And then we go anyway, even if we are scared."

Zora glanced back at me with a smile. "I know you do. I know you go anyway, even though you're scared. And you're right — watch that root sticking out — it doesn't make you a scaredy-cat. It makes you brave."

"Hm!" I doubted that, but it was nice to hear her say so.

"But you think I'm never scared, and that ain't true neither."

"You scared? I'd like to see that!"

"I'm scared plenty. It's just not that important to me, being scared."

We reached the towering canebrake that marked the southernish boundary of Mr. Polk's land. Mr. Polk was the town mute, and our friend. No one knew how old he was, but it wasn't a day under sixty. He lived alone with his horses. And he took a pride in them same as most other folks took pride in their children. People came from all around with their horse troubles, donkey troubles, mule troubles, and Mr. Polk helped them, one by one. He didn't talk with hand signs except to raise his palm for *Stop!* whenever someone tried to explain to him what the problem was. Most folks knew better than to try. They just brought their animal in, let Mr. Polk take it, and came back in a few days to pay—money, for some folks, but mostly whatever they could pay in, chickens, salt meat, vittles, what have you.

In terms of sheer acreage, Mr. Polk was the biggest landowner in town. His little cabin, the paddock and stables, and the big pasture behind them took up maybe four or five acres at least, and behind them sat a few hundred acres of overgrown woodland that went all the way to the resort town of Winter Park, and it all belonged to Mr. Polk. Folks in Eatonville gave the land no never-mind, since, thick with giant cane, all manner of pines, and knotty scrub brush, it offered nothing and enticed no one.

As we neared the cabin, we saw a shape crouched on the ground. Zora sprinted over, me at her heels.

There, right in front of his cabin door, doubled in half, was Mr. Polk. We knelt beside him, and the smell of burning cedar reached my nose.

"Mr. Polk," I cried, "something's burning in your cabin!"

I ran into his one-room abode. A small eating table was overturned, and a kerosene lantern, lying on its side, had begun to burn the straw mat that covered his earthen floor.

I couldn't stamp out the fire barefoot, so I grabbed

the quilt from his bed and smothered the flames. Within a minute, all that was left of the small fire was smoke strong enough to burn my eyes.

I pushed open the door and the single window and went back outside. Zora had helped Mr. Polk prop himself against the cabin wall. He was holding his left arm, and even in the dark we could see it was bleeding through his shirt, the blood pooling onto the fabric of his pants. He tried to stand but sank down again.

"Hold his hurt arm," Zora commanded.

In a heartbeat I was on his other side. I put my hand flat on his chest. "Mr. Polk, we're here." He was so thin I could feel his heart flutter like a butterfly wing under my palm. He nodded to me.

Zora offered him her shoulder and he pulled himself to his feet, with her supporting him under his good arm and me helping him cradle the wounded one. He stepped toward the cabin door. A last flicker of lightning lit up his face, making invisible all the wrinkles of age for a fraction of a second and revealing the face of a troubled boy.

"It's still smoky in there," I said, but Mr. Polk shook his head and we all went inside.

He sat on his bed while we found and lit a lantern.

Its light revealed a long, jagged wound running down the side of Mr. Polk's left arm. The fabric of his shirt was torn the length of the wound. All three of us stared. I couldn't imagine how he could have hurt himself so badly.

Zora suffered no such limits of the imagination. "You've been cut, Mr. Polk. Someone cut you." As she uttered the words, their truth was undeniable. Now that I knew it was intentional, his wound looked worse.

A shadow fell across the doorway. We looked up to see Old Lady Bronson. She was wrapped in a dark-gray shawl, her giant black cowhide bag hung against her right hip. With soldier boots that stopped below her knees and the dissipating smoke rising around her, the town conjure woman looked every bit the part of a witch. The steel-gray hair I'd only ever seen her wear in a single tight braid down her back blew wild behind her, gleaming with droplets of rain. Her freckled skin glowed in the lamplight. Silhouetted against the lightning-filled sky, Old Lady Bronson looked electrified.

She took in the situation with one sweep of her piercing black eyes, set her giant bag on the ground, and started pulling things from it.

"Carrie Brown and Zora Neale Hurston, don't just stand there. Fetch me a basin of water and some rags."

The presence of a grown woman, especially one with healing power, pushed away some of my fear. Zora and I set about collecting what she needed. I set the basin of clean water beside her, and Zora handed her a white shirt made of rough linen, the only cloth we could find in the little home.

Old Lady Bronson's wrinkled and arthritic hands belied their strength: she ripped the shirt as easy as shucking corn.

We watched her clean the wound and tie it closed with the strips of cloth. Then she pulled out of her bag a spool of silk thread and a crescent-shaped needle, which she quickly threaded and ran in circles over the gash faster than my eyes could follow, undoing each cloth strip as she reached it with a flick of her finger. It was clearly not the first time she had tended to such a stark wound. Mr. Polk watched her work. Other than the slightest wince as she pulled the thread taut, his face showed Old Lady Bronson nothing but tenderness. After tying off the last stitch and covering the wound in the last of the linen, Old Lady Bronson wiped the sweat from Mr. Polk's brow and placed a pillow stuffed with Spanish moss behind his back.

Mr. Polk took her hands in his worn and wrinkled ones. Then he turned his crinkled face to her and did the impossible: the town mute began to speak. Just like that, he opened his mouth and sound came out of it. Except that the sounds that flew out of his mouth made no sense to me. At first I didn't even recognize them as words; they were light as birds and so full of feeling. As he spoke, tears ran down the creases of his face.

Old Lady Bronson nodded as if she understood his sounds perfectly, as if he were speaking in plain English. Were we witnessing a miracle? It was as if Mr. Polk's wound had given him the gift of speech, but he spoke in a secret language only Old Lady Bronson could understand. Zora must have felt the same way, because she reached for my hand and held it tight. Neither of us uttered a word.

And then the conjure woman did something that surprised us as much as Mr. Polk's suddenly gaining the power of speech: she spoke back to him in that same strange tongue. She spoke slowly, each word weighted with what I took for sorrow, and her words seemed to calm him. He nodded, and then he looked deep into her eyes, his soul bared. I shivered.

Old Lady Bronson patted Polk's leg and stood up. "I'll be back with salve after daybreak. Rest up till I get back." Speaking English again seemed to remind her that Zora and I were still there, and she turned her stern gaze on us.

"Since you two little pitchers have the biggest ears in Eatonville, I'm sure you've taken this all in." Her words were a statement of fact, not a question. "And since you're grown enough to find yourselves here, I expect you to be grown enough to keep this to yourselves. All of it."

My lips parted in protest, and she silenced me with a gesture of her hand, but Zora would never oblige so easily.

Old Lady Bronson was a small woman with a big presence, and Zora stood only half a head shorter than her. Raising herself up to her full height, she looked almost eye to eye at the witch. Old Lady Bronson extended her hand and perched her slim fingers on Zora's shoulder. I would have screamed to have her touch me, but Zora didn't even flinch. She just went on looking her in the eye.

"How did you two come to be here, anyway? I know it wasn't Carrie Brown's idea to come strolling out way past midnight—and with a storm threatening, no less."

I bobbed my head in agreement, eager to get Zora out of the conjure woman's clutches and both of us back on the road toward home.

"Two of Mr. Polk's horses ran through my yard," Zora answered calmly. "We knew something was wrong."

Old Lady Bronson raised her eyebrows. "I always tell folks that twelve is a changeling year, and it looks like you starting to have some sense with your twelve years. You did right to come and check on Mr. Polk, but now it's time for you to go home and forget about all this."

"So who attacked him?" Zora acted as if she hadn't heard a word.

Old Lady Bronson tightened her grip on Zora's shoulder and leaned in. "Child, you are nobody's fool. And you tell a tall tale better than half the grown men in this town." She smiled just a little. "But this ain't no tale I want told."

There wasn't a grown-up alive who could stay

Zora's curiosity once it had been piqued, not even Mr. Hurston with a fresh-cut peach hickory in his hand. Old Lady Bronson was no exception.

"Miz Bronson, I don't want to tell nothing you don't want told, but Mr. Polk is our friend and I want to know what happened to him. How can he talk all of a sudden?"

I practically swallowed my tongue to hear Zora speak like that to the scariest person we knew, but she was as nonchalant as if she had just asked the time.

Old Lady Bronson's eyes flashed fire. "Child, you have mistaken me for someone who is bound by the everyday. Folks far and wide would travel a long way to avoid courting my temper."

Her tone made me ready to abide by any command she made. Not Zora. She stood there cool as a July cucumber.

"I just want to know the truth!" said Zora.

The old witch cocked her head. "I'll make you a deal, Zora." Her tone was softer than before. "You keep a lid on your pot till I tell you to lift it off. In return for your discretion, I will tell you a story worth hearing."

Zora's eyes widened at the prospect. "Will it have hoodoo and magic?"

"You just worry about keeping up your end of the bargain. I'll give you all the story you could ask for."

Her glance took us both in, and that rattled me. I most certainly did not want to hear her story or know any more about her hoodoo ways than I already knew! Zora, however, was over the moon. If there was one thing she couldn't resist, it was a deal traded in the currency of story. Her eyes lit up like shooting stars. She spit in her hand and held it out to Old Lady Bronson.

If that took the conjure woman by surprise, she didn't show it as she gave Zora her hand in return.

On the way home, Zora bounced like she had springs in her feet. "I wonder how long we got to keep quiet about this. You think a week? A month? And, mind you, just 'cause Old Lady Bronson told us not to tell anyone else, that don't mean we can't speculate between us. What do you think happened in there? I know you're thinking something."

I wanted to share in her excitement, but I just couldn't. The secret Mr. Polk shared with Old Lady Bronson didn't excite me; it frightened me. "Honestly, Zora, maybe it ain't for us to know. Maybe there's some secrets folks just ought to keep."

21

She looked at me incredulously. "Carrie Brown, you can't be serious. How on earth are we gonna suck the marrow out of life if we just sit by and let questions stroll down our street without inviting them in for a glass of lemonade? Mama always says, 'Ain't no one ever got dumber trying to answer a question.' And I intend to answer all life's questions. Anyways, Old Lady Bronson made me a deal. If we don't tell, she tells us a story."

I reached out and grabbed her hand. "You made a deal with the town witch. She's as likely to cast a spell on us as tell us a story. Ain't nothing free when you dealing with folks who talk to the living and the dead!"

Zora laughed at me. "You're just letting lowly Sir Coward get the best of brave Dame Courage. Old Lady Bronson won't hurt us. Besides, we're the ones who found her when she fell fishing by the Blue Sink. She's got no reason to cast hoodoo on us."

"Maybe..." I said slowly. "But I don't want to know things folks don't want me to know. Just like I don't want them to know things I don't want them to know!"

Zora kicked a stone down the road and started walking again. She was quiet, but I knew it wasn't because she agreed with me. Mr. Polk was our friend, and Zora understood friendship as a pledge made up of equal parts loyalty and honesty. She wasn't going to put the matter out of her mind until she had answers.

She put her arm in mine. "Maybe it's because I don't really have secrets. You know how my mind works — once a question starts a fire inside me, I have to answer it, no matter how bad I get burned. There ain't no pain more painful than the pleasure I get from the light of truth."

If I carried a secret right then, it was fear that my friend's curiosity would show her that some pain couldn't be lessened, no matter how bright the truth shined.

CHAPTER TWO

"Come on, Carrie. Daylight's tired of waiting for you."

I woke up to Zora shaking my shoulder. For a second I thought she had two heads, until I realized the other one belonged to Everett, who was riding on her back, grinning. I sat up, even though everything in me wanted to go back to sleep. "Don't look like daylight even knows its way here." Outside, dark clouds were still threatening thunderclaps and heavy-driving rain, although not a drop was falling.

"Seriously, though. We got to go check on Mr. Polk as soon as we can get out of Mama's way. If we don't, we're not worth a lick of salt."

"I want a lick of salt!" Everett crowed. He was four now, but I had been holding him since he was born and I couldn't help but still see him as Baby Everett.

"You want what, now?" Mrs. Hurston came in from the landing, a big ball of bedsheets on her hip. "Carrie, what you still doing in bed?" She gave me a once-over. "You feeling poorly? You sleep OK?"

Zora, back of her mother's shoulder, widened her eyes at me.

"No, ma'am. Yes, ma'am. I slept fine."

"Oh, no you didn't," said Zora. "You were just complaining I keep pushing you off the bed all night! Mama, we're getting big and this little bed ain't growing with us."

Mrs. Hurston sucked her teeth. "You ain't any bigger than you was two nights ago, and Carrie didn't look all worn-out like this yesterday morning. I think she's coming down with something. . . ."

That was my signal to wake up on the double. "No, ma'am!" I popped my eyes open and plastered on a big old smile. "Zora just woke me out of a dream, but I feel real good!" I sprang out of the bed like popping corn just to prove my words, still smiling like a fool.

That got me a sideways look. Mrs. Hurston set the ball of sheets on the bed, sat down, and motioned Zora over to the floor in front of her for the morning hair ritual. "You two about the worst fibbers I ever met. If you're gonna stay up half the night jibber-jabbing about Lord knows what, you can leastways have the decency to be honest about it."

"Yes, ma'am." We both lowered our heads with the shame we really did feel about lying, even though— or especially because—it wasn't the lie she thought it was. But neither of us set her straight. I reckon we figured lying to Zora's mama was safer than breaking our word to a witch.

"I want a lick of salt! I want a lick of salt!" Everett had turned his silly demand into a song and was bouncing around the room with it, occupying himself without our help.

Mrs. Hurston quickly rebraided Zora's hair for the day.

Lucy Hurston had a big litter of children, from little Everett up to Bob, who no longer lived in hailing distance, but I doubt any of them ever felt the sting of having to share their mother. Whenever one of them caught her attention, her focus was undivided. I was happy to catch some of that love shine when my own mama was away. It eased the homesickness I felt every time she had to leave me for more than a day.

Finished with Zora's hair, she gave me an appraising look. "Your hair need fixing, too, Carrie?"

"No, ma'am!" I answered with a sprightliness I definitely did not feel. I smoothed my ruffled head before her nimble fingers found their way into it.

"All right, then. You girls feed the hens and then help Sarah knead dough for the biscuits." She picked the sheets up under one arm, grabbed Everett under the other, and escorted Zora's youngest sibling back down to the main room.

"No," Everett was shouting. "Zora promised me a lick of salt! Zoraaaaaa!"

Zora pulled a clean dress over her head. "Wanna split my chores? We'll get done faster that way." I nodded, running my hands over the wrinkled front of my dress. I ran some grease from the jar on the dresser over my knees and gave my dress one last halfhearted tug.

"And keep those eyes looking bright," she said. "At least until we get out of Mama's sight!"

"I'm trying," I said.

"Try harder," she said, then she pinched my arm hard and ran down the stairs, me close behind to pinch her back.

Sarah was at the foot of the stairs, lying in wait for Zora. "Mama says you're supposed to help me with the biscuits! What took you so long?" Zora pulled a face behind Sarah's back and I headed out to feed the hens.

Sarah was a backward mirror of Zora. Where Zora was bold and honest like a bumblebee asking to nectar on springtime flowers, and loud and fearless like a bobcat, Sarah was quiet and calculating, demure and ingratiating, already versed in pleasing for the sake of winning other people's favor. The apple of her father's eye, she was everything Zora's father thought a girl should be. Zora was everything but.

With the chickens clucking around me, pecking frantically at the seed, I wondered how it would be to have a sister so different from me. I could see why my friendship meant so much to Zora. Unlike with Sarah, our differences complemented each other. Zora was always searching for new worlds, and when she couldn't find them, she made them up, while I was content to stay in one world and share it with Zora. I was enlivened by the new worlds Zora made, and she was comforted by the familiarity of mine.

The chickens were done feeding, their feverish pecking followed by an aimless and sated meandering.

I scattered my last handful of seed in a circle around me and walked back to the kitchen.

I heard Zora before I saw her. "Tattletale should be your middle name!"

"Don't act holier than thou with me, Zora Neale." Sarah always added the Neale when she was lording something over Zora. "I know you're up to something, and you best cut it out before I tell Daddy."

I walked in to see Zora sticking her tongue out at Sarah ferociously.

"Zora Neale Hurston! I will not tolerate ill-bred children in my house." It was Mr. Hurston, walking out of his bedroom and adjusting his workday suspenders. "Instead of telling Sarah about her business, you best be keeping your own business on the straight and narrow. As it is, you more trouble than a runaway mule!"

"I'm sorry, Daddy! I didn't mean to make trouble." Sarah was, as always, quick to play herself up in her father's presence.

Not Zora. She looked her father dead in the eye. "I'll try not to be a mule, Daddy; although, if I am, I know Mama won't want to be the donkey half of my parents."

I couldn't help noticing that what put her father

so often at odds with her was their sameness, not their difference. A storytelling preacher with a restless nature, who, in spite of being one of the most in-demand citizens of Eatonville, opened another congregation up in Sanford, over in Seminole County. One church wasn't enough for Mr. Hurston any more than fitting the mold of the "good daughter" was enough for Zora.

Mr. Hurston flashed with rage just as his wife stepped into the room. "That's right, John Hurston. If you call my child a mule, it's 'cause I'm the one who went and married a donkey."

Mr. Hurston muttered, "Lord have mercy," sat down, and stuck his nose in the family Bible. Mr. Hurston might have believed himself the thunder of righteousness in the Hurston home, but we all knew that it was quiet and steady Mrs. Hurston who was the law. When her protection enveloped her favorite child, not even John Hurston could touch Zora.

Mrs. Hurston fished a nickel from her apron and handed it to Zora. "You two go get me a cone of salt from Joe Clarke's store. And while you're at it, you can pick up a few more nails for your brother John to fix the henhouse."

John, who had been lost in the Sears catalog, sat

upright. "But, Mama, I was fixing to go fishing with Buford at the Blue Sink!"

"John, if a weasel gets in my henhouse again, you'll be out there guarding it yourself come nightfall. Be grateful I don't send you to get the nails, too."

Zora usually got on well with her older brothers, and she felt John's pain. "We'll help you, John. You'll be done in no time and still have plenty time for fishing."

"That's right, John," scoffed Mr. Hurston, "let your sister do your work. Just be careful you don't find yourself working for her one day!" He laughed loudly at his own joke.

I watched the comment slowly work its way under John's skin. "Aw, forget it, Zora," he said. "I don't need your help. Girls just get in the way!"

Zora's nostrils flared. "John, you'd be lucky if I let you work for me! Everyone should have a boss who's smarter than they are. You might even finally learn a thing or two!"

John jumped to his feet. "You can't talk to me like that! Mama, tell her she can't!"

"I'm just giving you right back what you gave me — only I'm so sweet I stopped to put a nice shine on it first. You can thank me later!" She grabbed my hand, grinning. "Come on, Carrie. We got chores to do!" Then we were flying out the door, Mrs. Hurston's laughter ringing behind us.

Zora skipped out the gate, then broke into a run. "Faster we get to Mr. Clarke's store, faster we get to Mr. Polk. And John can go suck an egg while he's waiting on those nails!"

Coming up the dusty road to Mr. Joe Clarke's porch, we saw a fine horse and wagon out front, the kind we usually saw only in Lake Maitland or Winter Park, or just passing through. It being fairly early yet, the porch had only three men instead of the usual full afternoon chorus. There was Mr. Chester Cools, Mr. Bertram Edges, and Mr. Luke Slayton.

"How much you want to bet that wagon cost way past a hundred dollars brand-new?"

"Come on, Luke. There ain't no wagon worth a hundred dollars, no how. I don't care how shiny they make it."

"Are you kidding me? The harness alone had to cost twenty-five dollars if it cost a penny!"

"Tell you what, if I had twenty-five dollars, I would not be spending it on no harness!"

"Why, hello, girls!" Mr. Cools, who had a little

farm out by the railroad tracks, always greeted us with a big old grin.

"Morning, Zora. Morning, Carrie," said Mr. Slayton. "What you think of my new horse and buggy? I just bought 'em for two hundred silver dollars — and that was a bargain!" Mr. Slayton could see the funny side of anything and anyone, make you laugh at yourself or him or both, and splash cold water on a hot temper about to combust. Unfortunately, he mostly needed to use that power when tempers were about to combust on him. Mr. Slayton was an incorrigible gambler. He would bet on anything just for the thrill of betting, and, like as not, he'd pick the losing gamble. He owed money to near on every man in Eatonville. When one of his creditors got to where he wouldn't be put off another day, Mr. Slayton would borrow money from a more patient creditor to pay him off. He had four kids, all small and skinny as scarecrows because, no matter how much Mr. Slayton worked, his pay never seemed to make it all the way home. And then there was poor Mrs. Slayton. We called her that because she was married to Mr. Slayton and had to raise four scarecrows on account of his bad ways. She was as silent as he was voluble; the only words we ever heard her say were "I thank you for your kindness," which she said every time someone couldn't stand the thought of her and those kids wasting away and had brought her a tin of milk or a sack of cornmeal or a hunk of fatback. When Mr. Slayton's sense of humor wasn't enough to stay the anger of an impatient creditor, it was probably only the thought of poor Mrs. Slayton and the scarecrow kids that kept him from getting rode out of town—or worse.

Mr. Edges, the town blacksmith and mechanic, was the only man in Eatonville who was serious all the time. If you said, "Hot as the devil today, ain't it, Mr. Edges?" he would stop what he was doing, think on your words, and say something like, "It is hot. I grant you that." Leaving you to fill in for yourself the rest of the thought: *Well, now, "as hot as the devil." Now, that's just an exaggeration, obviously* . . . He and Mrs. Edges never had kids, but they were sweeter to us kids than any parent, and they were probably responsible for half the vittles that made their way to poor Mrs. Slayton's table.

Mr. Slayton now regaled us with the details of his imagined wealth.

"See this horse?" Mr. Slayton said to us. "This is an Arabian horse. I had it shipped to Eatonville straight from Arabia."

Mr. Edges shook his head at such foolishness.

But Mr. Cools was smiling, playing along. "How you do that, Luke? You ship it in your private boat?"

"Oh, no, Mr. Cools." Zora couldn't resist jumping into the tall-tale telling. "There's only one way to ship as fine an animal as Mr. Slayton's."

Still happy to take the bait, Mr. Cools said, "Is that right, child? And what might that be?"

"Well," said Zora, barely holding back her own laughter, "by Pony Express, of course!"

We all bust out laughing, but just then a loud voice carried out to us from inside the store.

"You leave me no choice, boy!"

The screen door slammed open and a white man stormed out. His face was bright red and as wrinkled as parchment paper, except for a shining bruise on one cheek. His hair was limp and dingy white. He was so quick we didn't have time to move. He took the four steps from the porch in two, shoving Zora out of the way as he went. She stumbled into me but didn't fall. The man climbed into his fancy buggy and grabbed the reins so violently that the horse neighed in protest.

Joe Clarke had followed the man out onto the porch. "I believe we can talk this through—" he was saying.

"The time for talking is over," growled the man, not even looking at Mr. Clarke. "William, come!" he barked.

Behind Mr. Clarke, another white man, some years younger, came out of the store. "Sorry, Marshal," he said to Joe, smooth as oil, "but my client's rights are being repudiated." Mr. Clarke held up his hand to speak, but the man continued. "I'm here to help see that he gets his due, and no colored mayor"—he paused to laugh, softly but grimly—"will obstruct that."

He climbed into the wagon, and the older man said, loudly enough for everyone on the porch to hear, "This was a fool's errand!" He cracked the whip, and the horse took them off in a hurry, in the direction of Lake Maitland.

It was unusual to see white folks in Eatonville, even more unusual to see them exchanging angry words with Mr. Joe Clarke, our mayor and town marshal.

Mr. Clarke's usual demeanor was ebullient and cheerful. He was bigger than life to us. He especially liked Zora and never missed a chance to pit her wit against the wits of the men who frequented his porch. Today was an exception to the rule; his brow was furrowed.

Mr. Cools shot a stream of tobacco juice over the side of the porch. "Smells like trouble, Joe."

Mr. Clarke was about to reply when he noticed me and Zora. "Not now," he said to the men. Whatever he might have shared with the men on the porch, he suddenly decided was not for our ears.

Zora didn't care. "Who was that, Mr. Clarke? What were they so angry about?"

Mr. Clarke cut his eyes toward Mr. Cools, Mr. Slayton, and Mr. Edges, at a loss about how to answer her questions.

This made Mr. Slayton laugh. "You best watch out, Joe. Zora's about the finding-outest person in this whole town. She probably already knows more about this than you do, and she just got here!"

Mr. Clarke cracked a small smile.

"I don't like to brag, Mr. Clarke," Zora said, "but it's true; I am pretty good. And me and Carrie here — you know you can trust us with a secret." She gave him a serious look, and I knew she was thinking about that time we solved a murder, back when we were in fourth grade.

Mr. Clarke's face got serious again. He pulled up a chair and sat so his eyes more or less met ours. "Listen, girls. I do trust you, as much as I trust anybody in this town, and more than some." He shot a meaningful look at Mr. Slayton when he said this.

"Aw, now, Joe . . ." Mr. Slayton complained.

"But this is a situation I've got to think on. I've got to think on it hard before I tell another soul. Now, what your mama need this morning?"

Mr. Clarke ushered us into the store, attended to our purchase, and ushered us back out. On top of the parcel that held a paper cone of salt and a smaller one of nails, he placed a roll of colored candy wafers to fortify us on the way back.

As we were leaving, we heard Mr. Slayton murmur, "So what's this all about, Joe?"

Mr. Cools added, "Just between us menfolk."

"Y'all just heard me say I got to think before I talk," said Mr. Clarke. "Y'all think you the exception?"

"Aw, now, Joe . . ."

"Come on, Joe . . ."

Zora opened the waxy paper roll and popped a pink sugar wafer into her mouth. She sucked the candy thoughtfully. "So, Carrie, what you reckon that was about?"

"Darned if I know." After last night's events,

this was doubly unsettling. But what unsettled me enlivened Zora.

"Joe Clarke is about as shut-mouth as Mr. Polk and Old Lady Bronson. This town's just spilling over with secrets." Her smile got a little wider. "And I mean to be there to catch the overflow. Now, let's go check on Mr. Polk!"

CHAPTER THREE

W̲e were halfway to Mr. Polk's place when
Teddy Baker rounded the bend in the
road, in the buckboard his older brother
Micah was driving.

My heart beat a funny little rhythm when I saw
Teddy. Zora and I had been digging in the dirt and
sand, swimming in the Blue Sink, and climbing trees
with him since we could say our alphabets. I can't
remember a time we weren't together like three tight
buds on an inkberry branch. Lately he'd been taking
heat from other boys when he chose our company over
theirs at recess or when he passed up playing baseball

to listen to one of Zora's madcap schemes. Just turned thirteen, he was now taller than me and just half an inch over Zora, who until then had been the tallest of the three of us. We all seemed so different from how we'd been just a year ago. All kinds of strange, prickly, and warm feelings were overtaking me these days; the strangest were my feelings for Teddy.

He jumped off the buckboard, smiling brightly. "What y'all doing out here this morning? Don't Mrs. Hurston got you doing chores?"

Zora laughed. "We doing a chore right now, Teddy Baker."

Teddy glanced at Zora's paper parcel and the roll of candies. "Uh-huh. Going to Mr. Clarke's store ain't never a chore to you, Zora."

"Say, Lothario," Micah yelled from the buckboard, "you coming back with me, or you staying here with your two wives?"

Teddy rolled his eyes and slapped the back of the wagon. "Go on," he said. "I'll be home before supper."

Micah whistled. "Ladies, the only way to share him is to cut him in half. It's what King Solomon would do!" He pulled a face serious as a judge, and we all had to laugh. At seventeen, Micah was the spitting image of his father—tall, with kind eyes and a cinnamon complexion, sunburned from plowing fields every day in the hot sun.

Our feet took us to our favorite meeting spot, under the shade of Zora's favorite tree. According to Zora, the graceful old pine bent down its canopy of thick green branches to shade our three heads, and it laid down soft beds of pine needles especially and only for us three. She called it the Loving Pine, and we spent many an afternoon under it telling stories and pondering life. Her feelings for that tree were so deep they rubbed off on us. Teddy and I felt the same love for its rough bark and prickly needles as she did.

Teddy stretched out on the ground and smiled lazily up into the thick branches of the Loving Pine. That smile put a jarful of butterflies in my stomach, and, wanting to turn his gaze on me, I asked Zora, "Should we tell him?"

That made him sit up. "Tell me what?"

Old Lady Bronson had told us not to breathe a word about what happened at Mr. Polk's, but surely telling Teddy was not the same as telling grown folks. Besides, Teddy had a special relationship with Mr. Polk; he was the only other person he would let tend the horses. And if anyone could ease his mind about his horses, it would be Teddy.

Everyone who knew Teddy knew about his plan to be a veterinarian. Teddy took every chance he could to spend time with people who knew more about animals than he did. Since no one knew horses better than Mr. Polk, last June Teddy asked Mr. Polk if he could spend the summer helping him out whenever he wasn't needed on the farm. Mr. Polk, who had never worked with anyone as far as we knew, said yes—or, rather, he didn't say no, and he also didn't say no when Teddy asked if he could bring his best friends to watch sometimes. That was how we ended up spending a good part of the summer perching on an outer ring fence and watching Mr. Polk train the newest acquisition to his personal stable. It was a chestnut stallion from Ocala named Moss Star, and Teddy narrated for us everything we saw.

Mr. Polk had a gift for training horses that others gave up on or called impossible, untamable, or even ruined. We saw him do it with Moss Star. Moss Star had kicked a stable boy up in the air like a rag doll, and the only reason the owner wouldn't put him down was that he had "spent too much money to see a bullet bleed it all away." Instead, the owner traded Moss Star to Mr. Polk for a tame mare.

The first day, Mr. Polk let Moss Star out into the ring and left him alone. He let the horse kick and run and buck and grunt and whicker for an hour, two hours, a whole morning, until the sun was straight overhead. And all that while, Mr. Polk was there, standing stock-still, hands at his sides facing out. Whenever Moss Star looked his way, he'd nod his head slowly, as if to say, *Yes. Yes, I understand. You are right to kick and buck. This is good.*

Then he opened the gate back to the stall, where fresh water and a pail of oats were waiting. After lunch, they'd do the same thing; the horse would exhaust himself and Mr. Polk would give his soft nods of approval.

The next morning started out as more of the same, but after the better part of an hour, Mr. Polk disappeared. You can believe Moss Star noticed it. He looked all around and raised a ruckus when he couldn't see him. Then, just when Moss Star was ready to break down the paddock gate, Mr. Polk reappeared — and he wasn't alone.

From the other side of the stable and into the outer ring he led old Juniper, with nothing more than a braided rope draped loosely around the horse's neck, the two of them just slowly strolling along. Polk wasn't ignoring Moss Star so much as concentrating on Juniper, but when their eyes did meet, he gave Moss Star that gentle nod. This was the routine for a few days, and then, just as Zora and I were getting bored, Mr. Polk did something different. He started shortening and alternating the sessions with Moss Star and Juniper throughout the day—until it was a half hour Moss Star, a half hour Juniper. Then, one day, maybe five days into this routine, Moss Star walked up to Mr. Polk and lowered his head, just as he had seen Juniper do so many times. Mr. Polk stroked Moss Star's neck and placed the rope ring gently over his head, and the two of them took their first walk around the ring. From that day on, there was nothing Moss Star wouldn't do for Mr. Polk.

Those summer days, Teddy studied everything Mr. Polk did—the hand gestures, the nodding, the tongue-clicking sounds he made to communicate commands. To tell the truth, I probably did, too. As long as we kept our distance, neither Mr. Polk nor Moss Star seemed to mind having observers.

After the third week, when Mr. Polk finished up a session with Moss Star, he'd wave us over, and we could actually pet the handsome animal on his sweaty flank. Finally, Mr. Polk handed Teddy the rope and let him cool Moss Star and return him to the stable. Mr. Polk would run a handkerchief under the brim of his hat to mop up the sweat. He'd offer us a drink from his canteen. In all the time I knew Mr. Polk, it never occurred to me that his silence might be a conscious choice, not God's design.

Not wanting to be solely responsible for breaking our word to Old Lady Bronson, I looked at Zora expectantly. "Well, tell him!"

"Yeah," Teddy demanded, "tell me!"

"But we gave Old Lady Bronson our bond of silence in exchange for a story."

"Old Lady Bronson?" Teddy marveled. "Why would you be making deals with that old roots woman?"

"You gotta swear to keep this a secret," Zora breathed, and she put her right hand on her heart and held her left index finger out for Teddy to hook. This was the way we'd made promises to one another for years.

Teddy hooked his finger with hers. "OK, now tell!"

"Mr. Polk can talk," she said.

Teddy looked at her like she had two heads. "What do you mean, he can talk?"

"Just that," she continued. "We heard him talk to Old Lady Bronson, same as we're talking right now — except in a language we never heard. He ain't mute; he just chooses not to speak!"

Teddy looked to me — I suppose to check if Zora might be pulling his leg.

"It's true," I said. "We both heard him."

Teddy sat dumbfounded. "But how did you come to hear him speak?"

Zora was on her feet in an instant. Her words drew pictures of what we'd done but made the pictures so vivid that I was living them anew. The night wasn't just late and wet. It was "the darkest hour of the night under the shadow of a looming tempest." We weren't just checking on Mr. Polk. We were "on a rescue mission to outwit Death, facing the dark forces of the devil himself." Old Lady Bronson wasn't just a conjure woman, but "a portal between the worlds of light and darkness." And Mr. Polk's wound deepened from a nasty cut to "a sword slash from an unknown foe."

When she was done, Teddy jumped to his feet and stared at us. "Stabbed!" I think I had managed to put away the magnitude of the violence done to Mr.

Polk until Teddy spoke that word. "Are you sure he's OK?"

Not wanting to see Teddy worry, I pointed out that Old Lady Bronson was who folks called *after* they saw Doc Brazzle. Where Doc worked medicine, Old Lady Bronson sometimes worked a miracle. There were no hands more adept at turning a breech birth or binding a limb after a mule kick. Had Mr. Polk suffered from appendicitis, Doctor Brazzle would have been my healer of choice, but for a wound to the body or spirit, Old Lady Bronson was the better bet.

A little relieved from worry, Teddy's mind went to the stables. "What about the horses? You think they're back?"

"Only one way to find out," Zora said, "and we're on our way there." I could tell that she was pleased as punch by Teddy's eagerness to return with us to the stage of the adventure.

As we took off, Zora shook the brown paper parcel with the nails for the chicken coop at me. "I bet John's really waiting on these now," she said with a grin.

WESTIN

—·—

1855

CHAPTER FOUR

I can remember the sharp taste of salt in the air. We stood in front of the ship at dawn, the day already hot. Prisca held my hand tightly and clutched her doll, Maria Luz, in her other hand. The gangway stretched before us like a bridge to nowhere.

The night before, Mama Sezelle had lain next to me. "Be a good girl, Lucia. Do as they tell you." A tear slipped from her eye. I had never seen Mama Sezelle cry. Her wrinkled face, brown like dried cacao seeds, was creased with sadness. My throat burned and hot tears rolled down my face.

"Why do I have to leave you? I don't want to go."

"You are an orphan, Lucia. You must go where you are wanted."

"But don't you want me?" I cried.

"Of course I do, child, but it is not my place to keep you. You are of my heart, but not my blood."

I wrapped my arms around her, pressed my face into her warmth, and cried. "Remember," she said, stroking my face, "the trees speak, the birds speak, the plants speak, the land speaks. Listen and you will hear my voice."

Mama Sezelle was not my mother, but she had cared for me since my own mother died when I was almost three, taken by fever that consumed us both. When my mother passed, Mama Sezelle kept me alive. She fed me goat's milk and rice. Her work-worn hands showed me how to hold a spoon. My small hand grasped hers when I felt afraid.

Her little shack was my world: the white light from a full moon glowing through our one window, bats sailing across the night sky, the thin sheet quilted with birds stitched on in red and yellow and green, our wooden table with a mortar and pestle, the thick wooden mixing bowl only for *ceremonias sagradas.*

Mama Sezelle cooked for Don Federico and we lived behind his house. Every morning I would enter the kitchen with Mama Sezelle. I would hold her skirt while she cut onions, and I let the tart fragrance sting my eyes. I would wash the rice with water in a large tin bowl, removing every brown grain. I would watch Mama Sezelle's fast hands as she peeled and pulped *guanábana* for its sweet milky white juice.

In the early afternoon I would sneak behind the breakfront in Don Federico's library and listen to the lessons Prisca, his daughter, took while Don Federico read his beloved books. Afternoons were always natural science, French, and geography. I loved them all, but I especially liked when Prisca's tutor, Señor Mercedes, would ask her to stand in front of "the world as we know it," a beautiful globe nearly as tall as Prisca herself, and recite the countries, their capitals, their rulers. After he left and Don Federico went to take his siesta, Prisca would beckon me in. We would spin the globe and slap our hands to its smooth surface, declaring ourselves the princess of whatever dominion held still beneath our fingers: Cathay, the Argentine, the Kingdom of Congo . . . In the late afternoon, thirsty and filled with mischief, we would seek out Mama Sezelle in her kitchen. Prisca would laugh and pick hot plantains from the frying pan, Mama Sezelle slapping her fingers away. She would grab my hand and pull me into the garden, a sea of flowers and lime trees stretching a long way before the corner of the shack that Mama Sezelle and I lived in became visible.

We made up songs in Spanish, and in the French I couldn't help learning. We carefully lifted wasp nests that had fallen from tamarind branches and restored them to their perches. We made dolls from unripe cashews, each brown seed a cap for their green heads—doll babies nestled to our bosoms. We were inseparable, both having lost our mothers before memories of them could form. When we were smaller, I scarcely knew where my arm ended and hers began; we were so close we believed ourselves to be the dark and light versions of the same girl. We sang songs we learned and songs we made up, danced everywhere we went, read to each other, acted out stories, pretended to be wood nymphs running in and out of the lime trees or water sprites in the surf. Anything and everything we could think of, we did. The differences between us—she the daughter of a gentleman, me an orphaned serving girl—never bothered us. It was the natural order of things, not worthy of remark.

The night before I left, Mama Sezelle took the

bowl from the table. She spat in it and made me do the same. She lit a tallow candle and dripped the melted fat into the bowl. She prayed with words I barely understood. Words she spoke with the other older women of our town. Words they spoke when the whites had gone to sleep, when young mothers in hard labor needed strong hands to pull the newborns into this world, when suitors were scorned or lovers spurned.

Then she whispered in my ear, "Remember."

My legs shook as Prisca and I followed Don Federico into the stomach of the ship. Five days later it spat us out in a country called Florida, in a city called Saint Augustine. Here, Don Federico told us I would have to call him Master Frederic from now on. Here, he told us, he would join the widow who was to become his new wife, the woman he took us from our island to marry, the woman he promised Prisca would be the mother she had never had. Because I was an orphan, he had the power to bring me to Florida with them. And he took me because Prisca would not leave me behind.

In Florida everything looked, smelled, and sounded

different. Overwhelmed by homesickness, Prisca cried as a carriage drove the three of us from the ship to the house of a distant cousin.

That night, Prisca and I lay in bed. I listened for the sound of crickets, but even the insects sang in a strange new language there. I got up and went to the window. The moon was half full. My eyes looked over the garden and I saw two palm trees grown from the same trunk. Mama Sezelle said a split tree like that meant a house divided. I crawled back into bed, knowing we had done more than simply leave one place and come to another.

The next day everything moved quickly. In the small church we met Miss Caroline. She was small and round. Her eyes were quick, but they did not smile when her mouth did. She hugged Prisca and carefully put a new bonnet on her. Master Frederic told me to wait with the boy by Miss Caroline's carriage while the three of them went into a small church. The boy's skin was burnished in reds and browns, and his eyes took in everything. He spoke to me, but I could not understand his words. I smiled at him to hide my fear, and he smiled back. Thin and reedy, he looked to be eleven, like I was. He picked up a stick and drew the outline of a house in the sand. Then he pointed into the distance. I nodded, acknowledging that my future lay south of where we stood.

When Prisca, Master Frederic, and Miss Caroline returned, Master Frederic told me to sit in the front of the carriage on the driver's bench, next to the boy. The sun beat down on us as we rode over rough roads and through dense woods. A new jungle. Prisca called to me from inside the coach and I called back. We named the few flowers and birds we could recognize, we made up names for the others, and we sang. I became sleepy and almost fell from the narrow perch of the driver's seat. The boy grabbed me and set me right. He laughed, and I laughed with him. He gently linked his arm through mine so that when sleep overtook me again, I would fall against his shoulder.

At night we stopped in a town called Mellonville. Mosquitoes played angry music into the humid night air. I slept in a cramped bed next to Prisca. I bit down on my fist to keep from crying.

As soon as the sun showed itself, we drove still deeper south. It wasn't until nightfall had been with us several hours that we finally reached a house, lit from inside. The doors opened and two women appeared. They were several shades darker than me and dressed in dull linens worn from patching. Miss Caroline's voice became sharp, and they did her bidding with hurried steps.

Inside the house, the boy went to stand with the two women. Prisca and I stood together, Prisca holding my hand in hers. Miss Caroline and Master Frederic exchanged words, but I could not understand them. I looked to Prisca for help, but she just stared at the floor. My ache for Mama Sezelle, for home, was so strong I almost fell to my knees.

Miss Caroline stepped toward me, saying something. The more she said, the tighter Prisca gripped my hand. I stared into Miss Caroline's blue eyes, but all I could read in her face was displeasure.

She addressed Prisca then, who only shook her head. In our old language, Master Frederic told me to let go of Prisca's hand, even though it was Prisca who held me. I shook my head, too, full of confusion.

Miss Caroline spoke to Prisca again, her voice low and firm. Prisca still would not look at her. Miss Caroline came toward us and, with her small moist hands, pried ours apart.

Prisca cried out to Master Frederic, who did not respond. I felt a new kind of fear growing in me. I was in a place I would never choose to come, if choice were ever mine.

Miss Caroline called to one of the women by the door, who came and took me by the wrist. Miss Caroline led Prisca, me, and my keeper upstairs to a bedroom. In the room was a bed and, next to it on the floor, a straw-filled pallet. The room was lit by three candles casting long shadows on the walls. The woman who had led me by the wrist handed me a worn linen shift, a smaller version of her own. I realized I was expected to wear it. While the three of them watched, I undressed and put on the linen shift. It was rough, not at all like the smooth cotton of my own clothes. I had only a handful of dresses, but they were all pretty, each one something Prisca, who was two years older than me, had outgrown.

Miss Caroline pointed at the pallet on the floor, then at me. I stared. When I looked over at Prisca, she was crying. She ran to the door and called to her father, loud and insistent.

When Master Frederic appeared, his face wore no expression.

Prisca spoke to him in our language. "Why must they take away Lucia's dresses? And why would they have her sleep on the floor when the bed is more than big enough for the two of us?"

Master Frederic shrugged his shoulders. "My daughter, this is how things are done here."

"That is absurd," Prisca yelled with fury. "It is not how *we* do things! Lucia is not a dog!"

Miss Caroline had moved to stand close beside Master Frederic. She smiled at her new husband, then reached out and stroked Prisca's tearstained face, as if in sympathy. She then took Prisca's arm gently and led her to the door. Prisca glanced back over her shoulder at me as they took her from the room.

The woman who had taken my dress earlier pointed to herself. "Rebecca."

I pointed to myself. "Lucia."

She nodded and pointed to the straw pallet. She pointed to the bed and shook her head.

Then she blew out the candles and left.

All night I lay awake, dreading what further darkness the morning would bring.

Long after the first rays of sunlight had filled the room, Miss Caroline opened the door to find me sitting on the pallet, knees against my chest. She indicated that I should follow her out of the room and downstairs. On the ground floor, we walked down a hall past several rooms, one of them a library where Master Frederic sat at a long table with Prisca, reading. We passed through a small room that held many things for serving and eating, and out into a yard. In the yard was an outbuilding, which I would learn was the cookhouse. On the other side of the outbuilding's Dutch door stood Rebecca, the collar of her dress already rimmed with sweat from the heat.

The yard was neatly raked, and chickens were picking lazily in the weeds. And then I noticed, off to the side, a small pile of sticks and cloth: all I owned, all I had brought with me—my dresses and my shoes—jumbled up with kindling. The boy from the carriage stood by the pile, looking to Miss Caroline for a sign. Miss Caroline nodded and he went to the door of the cookhouse, where Rebecca passed him a flaming stick. He threw it on the pile and I watched my clothes burn. I looked up at him and he held my gaze. There was kindness in his eyes. Again he saved me from falling.

Once the pile had burned down, Miss Caroline walked back into the main house. I had been given my lesson.

As soon as she was out of sight, I stumbled over

to bushes brimming with white blossoms and emptied what little there was in my stomach. When I turned, the boy was behind me, holding something out to me. Frozen, I stared at him. He looked around carefully before taking my hand and pushing some soft fabric into it, then walked away. I opened my hand. It was a white handkerchief, carefully embroidered with a red flamingo. Prisca had received it as a gift and in turn gifted it to Mama Sezelle, who carried it in her pocket every day — until the night she packed it with my few belongings. The boy whose name I did not know had rescued a small piece of my past.

Moments later, Rebecca motioned for me to follow her into the cookhouse. There, I worked. I carried the wooden bucket to the well and filled it. I cut okra into thin slices. I salted and rubbed cast iron pans and swept the kitchen. In the afternoon, my chores did not end. Nor did Prisca come to see me.

That night, after the dinner was prepared and I had eaten my meager bowl of grits and corn bread by the fire, Rebecca motioned that I should go upstairs to bed.

I entered the room I'd been left in the previous night and found Prisca sitting on the bed, her bed.

Her eyes had blue shadows, and I guessed that, like me, she had not slept the night before.

We spoke in the language of our home.

"They do not allow me to play with you." Her voice was flat.

"Why not?" I asked.

"Because you are a slave now."

Only one time after that did she ever mention my condition again.

For the first two weeks, when the two of us were alone, I allowed myself the fantasy that things between us were as they had been, that we still could enjoy each other's company in a time and place without slavery. It was a useless fantasy and a dangerous one. The present was a hell with no escape, and the past could change nothing about that.

We had been at Westin for three weeks. My hands were raw from the heat of the laundry water and the lye we used to wash the clothes. At night after I had served and cleaned, and gotten the fireplace and kindling ready for the next day, I would climb the stairs to Prisca's room. My legs and arms hurt from the work, and I trembled with exhaustion. As soon as I entered the room, Prisca would beg me to read a fairy tale with her, then demand that we act it out. My eyes would blur the words on the page, and I would try to sit on my pallet whenever our play slowed down.

One night I told her it hurt my hands to hold the heavy book. She turned them over and looked at my palms. They were cracked and covered in broken blisters. She looked into my eyes, her face pale and empty. I tried to lie down.

"No," she hissed into the night. "You're Cinderella. And your wicked stepsisters have made you work until your hands bleed! But I am your fairy godmother." She went to her dresser, scooped out a fingerful of *pommade en crème*, and started rubbing it into my hands.

I yanked them away. "This is no story, Prisca. My hands hurt because they work me every hour that there is daylight!"

Prisca pushed back from me, then began to cry like a child. "I'm trying to help!"

I instantly regretted what I had said. Not for upsetting her, but for fear that Miss Caroline would hear. If she found Prisca crying, she would lay the blame on me and punish me for it. I had already been yelled at for not dressing Prisca quickly enough, slapped for taking too long to do a task, and pinched purple for dropping a saucer. I was terrified of what Prisca's tears could bring.

And so I shushed her, apologizing gently until her tears slowed.

In that moment I learned to be a slave even with Prisca. To bottle up my feelings and my fears so that she did not unleash the force of her own power, a power she herself barely understood. The power to be a whole person, her whole self, while I was now forced to exist as a fraction of a human being, a slave with no rights to my own self. What Prisca did not understand, but that I now did, was that the past meant nothing.

She answered me in a ferocious whisper. "Out there you're a slave, but in here we are as we always have been. In here, nothing has changed!"

That first year Prisca often pulled me into her bed during the night and wept onto my shoulder. I did not weep with her. I lay still, the flesh-and-blood doll she turned to when her loneliness became too hard to bear.

CHAPTER FIVE

It had been three years since I first came to Westin, the name they gave this farm in the Florida wilderness, and Master Frederic was dying.

Miss Caroline had at first denied the signs — he passed water in the night, the whites of his eyes were yellow, and his fingernails splintered. I said nothing, but Prisca watched me watch him. She knew that, having been raised by Mama Sezelle, I recognized the signs of death. Three years of living as a slave had altered me, however, and I had become adept at keeping my emotions and thoughts from betraying themselves on my face.

Prisca was sleeping, her brow and chest beaded in sweat. After all this time, we still shared a room—not because I had any say in the matter, but because Prisca demanded it. I walked to the window in the hopes of catching a slight breeze. In the fields, the other slaves were already in the cotton. There were sixteen of us altogether at Westin. Twelve worked the field full-time; three tended to the household and its needs. Between the house and the field was Horatio, the boy who sat next to me on our long trip to Westin, the boy who saved a small piece of cloth from fire. It had taken me three days to learn his name, six months to learn his language, and twelve months to teach him how to read simple sentences. Horatio was my best friend.

I watched him getting water for the horses, stooped under the weight of the two buckets, his thin frame a balance scale tilting from side to side.

I heard yelling from the field and wondered who Mr. Krowse, the overseer, was showing the whip to. As much as I feared the whip, today I imagined it could almost be better than the long hot hours waiting for death.

I poured water into the basin, and the sound woke Prisca. She sat upright. "Is he gone?"

I shook my head. She exhaled slowly and got out of bed.

"Do you want to wash?" I asked, pointing at the basin of fresh water. She shook her head and stepped into the same dress she had worn the day before, not waiting for me to button it, and left the room without another word.

I walked over to the basin and splashed cool water on my face. That's when I saw it: a peppered moth, coal black, perched on the dresser, its silvering wing dust glinting in the reflection of the glass. I had never seen one during the daytime before and never one so large. It was almost the size of my hand. The words of Mama Sezelle and the old island women came back to me. "An easy death brings rain, and a hard death brings an omen." Then I remembered what Mama Sezelle had taught me: fear is the absence of understanding; knowing the ways of the natural world is power. I remembered some of the stories and the legends the old women in my homeland told me. I remembered some of their ways: I made orange leaf tea to stop vomiting, bathed a scorpion bite in spruce tea, and applied a sweet potato root poultice on burns. But now I wished I had fought sleep harder and had listened more intently to the signs the old women spoke about in hushed voices on warm island evenings. Now more than ever I needed to understand their meanings.

I turned around and moved toward the moth, holding out my hand. It alighted on my finger as if accustomed to human touch. I gazed at it with wonder and a small shudder. An endless minute passed. And then, moving with the slow grace of a weighty bird, the peppered moth flew out the open window just as Prisca's screams began to reverberate through the house.

I ran downstairs, but stopped at the door to the drawing room.

Miss Caroline's grown daughter, Alice, was holding on to her, as if to comfort her. Miss Caroline's face was drawn, her pale-blue eyes rimmed with red. The faces of Miss Alice and her husband, Master George Peterson, by contrast, were somber but not grief-stricken. They looked as well-rested and easy as they had five months ago at Christmas. The Petersons' son, Timothy, a pale, thin version of his tall and dark-haired father, did not even look at his dead step-grandfather. His eyes instead searched the faces of his parents, as if he didn't know how he was supposed to react or to feel and needed to take his cues from them.

I found Prisca kneeling by her father's bed, a tumult of sheets. Master Frederic had given death a hard fight, but now his limp body and Prisca's weeping were all that was left of the battle.

Prisca was now an orphan, like me. I had spent my whole life with him and Prisca, but his death did not move me in the slightest. The only sorrow I felt at his dying was the sadness I felt for Prisca's loss of her father. I do not think a slave who has seen the power of the whip can truly sorrow for someone who owns people, no matter how benevolently he owns them. If there is a kindness that can soften the blow of stolen freedom, I have not seen it.

I moved toward Prisca, but the tight grip of Miss Alice closed around my arm. "Go cover the mirrors, girl," she said to me. So I left to gather white sheets.

The afternoon turned hot and humid, and the sickly-sweet smell of gardenias further choked the air. Prisca disappeared into her room while the drawing room was prepared and Master Frederic's body laid out with fitting dignity. When Miss Alice sent me up with cool water and buttered bread, I could hear weeping on the other side of the locked door, but she did not answer my knock.

Back in the cookhouse I helped Rebecca squeeze

lemons for lemonade and stuff blueberry pies. Rebecca was a small woman, half as round as she was tall, the color of dark maple syrup, with almond-shaped eyes that all but disappeared on those rare occasions when she laughed. She worked at a rapid pace, the sweat dripping from her brow.

The second my hands fell idle, she gave me a new task. "Snap beans need readying," she ordered, looking up at me. Then something beyond me caught her eye, causing her to gasp and take a step back.

I turned around to see that the peppered moth had lighted on the ledge of the bottom Dutch door, its wide black fan of wings stark against the thick ivory paint.

"Such a moth," she whispered, frightened.

The arrival of the moth was as arresting to Rebecca as it had been to me, but it did not frighten me as it did her.

Before I could reach the door, Timothy's voice rang out from the direction of the stables.

"Rebecca! Come! I'm thirsty and I want cool water!"

At fourteen he had already mastered the implicit threat of his father's commands.

He was coming toward the cookhouse. Across his

shoulder was slung the rifle he always carried, pressed tight against his lean frame like a second spine.

We reached the Dutch door at the same time, he on the outside and me on the inside. We both looked at the moth.

Startled, he hit at the creature blindly and the moth fell to the ground.

I called out "No!" just once, but I was too late. In one swift move, he had taken the rifle from his back and smashed the moth with its barrel. The moth no longer moved, but he struck it a second time and then kicked it away. He looked up then and I saw his face. It was red, as if with rage, but I recognized it as the mask of fear he often wore.

Rebecca pulled me roughly away from the door, invoked Jesus, and spit in the fire.

Timothy stared at us. "Rebecca, bring my water out front. I want to sit in the shade," he ordered, then reshouldered his weapon and walked off. Rebecca moved to obey his command.

Once he was gone, I went to where the moth lay and picked up its mangled body. It fluttered slightly in my hand, the last life leaving it. My fingers glowed with silver dust from its once-glittering wings.

EATONVILLE

1903

CHAPTER SIX

Mr. Polk's cabin sat at the far end of the paddock, straight and narrow like a skinny woman. Compensating for her lack of curves, the small house wrapped itself with star jasmine bushes, waving their bright petals like thin white handkerchiefs, and beauty berry bushes whose flowers danced. All the color and movement made a person forget that the house was no more than eight feet across and ten feet long—tiny enough to make Mama's and my three little rooms seem like a palace. Most of Mr. Polk's land may have been wild and uninviting, but the part he cultivated and tended for himself and his horses beckoned to the Florida sun to shine down love on it.

Teddy knocked softly. The man who answered was not the bloodied and disoriented soul we had found in the middle of the night before. Mr. Polk stood before us fully himself again. He was wearing fresh clothes and his arm was wrapped in a tight sling. Outwardly, there was nothing that a fall from a horse couldn't explain. Behind him the little cabin was tidy and welcoming, making it clear that Old Lady Bronson had indeed returned in the morning.

"Mr. Polk, are you doing all right?" Teddy asked. Mr. Polk nodded gravely and gave Teddy's hand a few reassuring squeezes. Teddy was visibly relieved to see his mentor in full possession of himself. Then he turned and looked over at the paddock, where four horses were grazing calmly, and his brow furrowed again.

"Where is Moss Star?" he asked.

Mr. Polk's mouth dipped at the corners with sadness. He shook his head and shrugged.

Teddy understood immediately. "He's lost," he said aloud. "He has to be lost, or he would have come back."

Mr. Polk nodded slowly.

Teddy looked around, considering the possibilities of where a frightened horse might go. With a large sweep of his arm, he motioned toward the expanse of thick woods beyond the rail fence that bordered Mr. Polk's pasture, the land folks called Polk's Woods. "What about back here?"

Mr. Polk bobbled his head back and forth, as if to say, *Maybe, maybe not; hard to say. . . .*

Teddy considered. "Well, we can go in and look for him, call to him. Maybe if he hears my voice he'll find his way back."

Mr. Polk pondered this for a moment, then gave Teddy one short nod. The three of us followed him to the stable, where he took the big, shaggy rope down from the outside wall and gave it to Teddy.

Teddy took the lead with the solemnity of a military honor and hung it across his shoulder. "I'll bring him home, Mr. Polk."

Mr. Polk patted each of us gently on the back, the way he might the neck of a good horse. It was his way of saying, *Thank you for bringing Teddy.* I was pretty sure that however much Mr. Polk valued his own life, he valued the lives of his horses more. No one understood that better than Teddy.

Beyond the split-rail fence, Mr. Polk's property

turned wild; a forest of tall pines, dense thicket, uncut cane, and rebellious scrub led you into deep shade. Daylight was there, but tall trees had conspired to shrink the sun's power, and the density of the dark was palpable. The land here wasn't merely fallow; it pushed back hard against any thought of cultivating it. Teddy led us farther in, keeping up a steady clicking and whistling, clearing our way by poking a long branch ahead of him to rout out any snakes. I could imagine anyone getting lost in here, not least a scared horse.

"Teddy," I said, slapping at mosquitoes and rubbing my branch-stung legs. "You think Moss Star is somewhere in all this? Don't seem like anything with sense would want to come back here."

Teddy looked grave. "He'd go home if he could, just like the others did. The only reason he wouldn't is if he was hurt." Teddy was rarely wrong about animals, and I realized that he and Mr. Polk were way ahead of Zora and me. It wasn't Moss Star being lost that concerned them. It was the possibility that he was hurt or worse.

For the next half hour, the three of us said little. We squeezed our way between trees and cane, trying to keep ourselves oriented. We came to some gritty sand, made soft enough by the previous night's drizzle to show hoof prints if there were any, but there was no sign of Moss Star. There was no sign that anybody, man or beast, had been back here for a long, long time.

Every now and then Teddy would kneel and touch the ground, pass his hand gently over pine needles and sand. Then he would shake his head and we would keep pressing forward. He broke a branch every few feet, marking our way back out at the same time he was looking for traces of Moss Star.

About the twelfth time Teddy knelt down, I was standing by, looking around, when I made out something so strange I thought at first that it might have been a mirage. I tapped Zora's shoulder and pointed. Teddy stood up, too, and when he saw what I was pointing at, let out a soft "Oh!" A few yards away from us, the woods engulfed a structure only two stories tall but imposing nonetheless. It was a sight that nature never put there.

House wasn't quite the right word. It was more like a shipwreck in the shape of a house. While the Hurston house was the biggest in Eatonville—even bigger than Doctor Brazzle's—you could have fit three or four of them inside this one. Big as it was, pines and cane and morning glory crowded around it so tightly that it was all but invisible until you were almost on its front steps. Not a drop of paint remained anywhere, and the wood, parched and bony or swollen with rot, matched the dishwater gray of the clouds overhead. Even the boards that covered every window and doorway were choked with dead vines swirling thick as serpents. If the house had been a head, it would have belonged to Medusa.

"What is it?" I asked.

Neither Zora nor Teddy answered as we approached it quietly, softly, as if it were a baleful spirit that might awaken if you startled it.

"Looks like an old ... house," Zora whispered into the eerie silence that surrounded the place.

Looking at it unsettled me — like we had some-how left Eatonville while still being in it.

"Not just a house," Teddy said, stepping back to take it all in. "This is a plantation house."

"A plantation house?" I squawked. "You mean from slavery?"

Teddy nodded. "The only folks who could have a house this big and this old would be white folks."

"You mean slave owners," Zora clarified.

The word *slave* hung in the air.

I tried to wrap my mind around it. "You think the folks who lived in this house owned slaves?"

Zora ran her hand across the moss growing on the north side of what remained of the porch beams. "Slaves," she said, drawing out the word. "The word makes the pit of my stomach burn. Whenever I think of slavery I get angry. No matter how long I study white folks, I'll never understand how so many of them could sit in big houses like this, *owning* folks who had no more say in their own lives than a dray horse."

"We're lucky we were born when we were," Teddy said. "Just forty years ago and we would have been slaves. Imagine us being us, only slaves."

"How do you think they bore it?" Zora asked. "How do you stand being owned by people who playact that there's a world of difference between you when there ain't no difference between folks past a few degrees of color? How you think folks stood being worked like mules?" With a gloomy look, she answered her own question. "I wouldn't have stood it. I would have run north!"

Teddy nodded, his mouth a grim line.

"But . . ." I groped for words. "What if you couldn't run with your whole family? Would you still go, thinking you might not ever see any of them again, ever?" I was thinking about how at one time I would have given almost anything to be with my father. I used to miss him so much that I would have been willing to die, too, just to be with him. In the end, it was loving my mother and Zora that ultimately kept me tethered to this life.

Zora's brow creased. "What a horrible choice: freedom for yourself or slavery with the folks you love."

Teddy shook his head and said, "Seems like no matter what you chose, running or staying, you must have had a broken heart your whole life."

We all chewed on that.

We couldn't imagine the sandy soil that bore the beauty of cape jasmine blossoms and yielded juicy oranges and grapefruit being worked by folks who looked like us yet were treated worse than animals. We knew about slavery, of course. Zora, Teddy, and I also learned in school that daring men like Robert Smalls and Martin Delany persuaded Lincoln to let colored men join the Union army. And there wasn't a child in Eatonville who couldn't recite the Gettysburg Address by heart. But despite what we'd learned at school, the outlines of slavery were blurry. Slavery happened to folks who lived in the past and somewhere else; our

Eatonville was a place where Negroes lived outside of the will of white folks, and we only ever saw ourselves as a bright future.

I spoke my next thought out loud. "You reckon anyone here in Eatonville was ever a slave?"

Zora thought for a second. "My daddy, for one. He always says he was born a slave in Alabama, but that soon as he could walk, he walked right on out to freedom."

I smiled because I'd heard Mr. Hurston say just those words. "He must have been just a baby, though. All our parents would have been babies by the time slavery ended. They wouldn't remember it beyond what folks told them."

"I reckon Mr. Polk's old enough to have been a slave," Teddy said. "Do you think he knows a plantation is sitting on his land?"

"Folks have always said there's nothing out here," said Zora. "Everybody except Mr. Polk, that is, because he ain't said nothing ever."

I fixed her a look. "So you reckon he knows this plantation house is here?"

"Carrie, it's like you said yesterday. Seems like half the things we thought we knew about Mr. Polk ain't at all what we thought."

"You think this house is a secret?" Teddy said, raising an eyebrow. "A secret Mr. Polk knows all about?"

I could see Zora's mind spinning like a pinwheel. "I suspect this is a whole *story*. Maybe it just *feels* like a secret because Mr. Polk can't tell his story. At least not in a language we can understand."

I shivered. It felt funny standing here on Mr. Polk's land, looking at this hull of a house. Everything about it raised questions, and I wondered if not speaking at all was the only way Mr. Polk could keep so much to himself.

CHAPTER SEVEN

A few heavy drops fell from the sky and we automatically looked toward the old plantation house, thinking it might offer us some measure of shelter.

"It ain't gonna rain," Zora said, testing the air with her hand. "These are just bluffing clouds and teaser drops."

But the drops grew heavier and faster, and we climbed the rickety front steps. Teddy took the steps two at a time and I followed close behind. My foot landed on the third step, but the wood was so rotten that my foot went clear through the board. Before I could pitch forward, Teddy grabbed me and pulled me up. His dark-brown eyes looked into mine. "You OK?"

I held his hand until I had both feet on the porch.

"Sure she's OK," said Zora. "You caught her just in time." She grabbed my hand now and pulled me toward the doorway. Aside from a tiny gecko scampering away from us, nothing moved.

I pulled my hand loose from Zora's. "I don't think we should go in. Honestly. The floor is rotted through everywhere."

"Just test your steps first," she said, doing nothing of the kind. She moved inside and was quickly out of sight, off to explore the rooms on the first floor.

I crossed the threshold and took a few tentative steps into the gloomy interior. Dust motes floated across beams of weak light filtering through broken window boards. Strips of what must have been wallpaper were peeling from the walls. The entrance was devoid of any furnishings or decoration. Standing there and looking around at the dark doorways to empty rooms, I felt as if I were in a crypt that even the corpses had abandoned. I turned around quickly to go back outside, not realizing how close behind me Teddy was, and turned right into his arms. We stood there, touching, not moving, his face close to mine. I froze and closed my eyes. Suddenly, Zora's voice echoed through the house. "You'll want to see this!"

I opened my eyes and stepped back. Teddy was laughing. "Carrie Brown, were you trying to kiss me?"

The pleasant warmth I had felt a moment ago turned into a hot flush. "Me, kiss you?" I hissed. "You were about to kiss me!"

Before Teddy could reply, Zora was walking toward us holding a rusty old rifle.

We spun away from each other and gave our full attention to Zora. At least Teddy did—I was pretending to, but inside I was fuming.

Zora shook sand and dust loose from the rusted barrel before holding it out to Teddy. When he didn't reach for it, Zora turned the rifle over in her hands. "How old do you think this is?"

"That's a musket. See?" He pointed to the end of the barrel. "You load it through the muzzle. It's gotta be at least as old as this house."

I could see the darker side of Zora's imagination taking wing. "You think they used it against slaves?"

The thought repulsed me, and I rushed to push it away. "Of course not. Somebody probably forgot it here during a hunting trip." But my words felt hollow, and neither Zora nor Teddy echoed agreement. I didn't believe it myself.

"You want it?" Zora asked Teddy, raising it to her eye and gazing down its barrel.

Teddy reached out and gently pushed the barrel of the gun down. "We got plenty rifles at home, and I don't want none of them, either."

Zora looked down at the gun dolefully. "I'm sorry I even picked it up."

I was sorry right along with her. The gun made the house feel like a cage set with a trap.

"Best thing you can do with that gun is bury it," Teddy offered.

I was still piqued by his antics after our near kiss, but his words sent a chill down my spine. I could see they left Zora unsettled, too.

"Don't try to spook her, Teddy," I said.

He looked at me, a smile playing at the corner of his mouth again. "Seems like you the only one I'm spooking today."

I felt the slow burn of embarrassment heating up

my face again. "I ain't paying no attention to you whatsoever!"

"What are you two talking about?" Zora looked between us with curiosity.

"Nothing!" I shoved past Teddy, stomped back out onto the porch to find the rain had stopped, went down the steps, and began to push my way through tree and shrub back toward Mr. Polk's cabin.

Behind me I heard Zora ask Teddy, "What did you do to her?"

"Me? I ain't done nothing!"

The last thing I heard before I was out of earshot was Zora saying, "Way you always teasing her, if I didn't know better, I'd think you were sweet on her."

I scowled and followed Teddy's broken-branch markers, getting far enough away that I couldn't see the old plantation house if I'd tried—and I wasn't trying. The air was cooler now, after the sprinkle of rain, with a soft breeze moving among the trees.

I could hear Zora and Teddy pushing their way through the pines behind me, and soon they were standing on either side of me.

"Hey, what are you—?" Zora began, but stopped as a strange crying sound reached our ears.

"Is that a hurt animal?" asked Teddy.

There was a big camphor tree and behind it a small clot of myrtle oak to the west of us, and the sound seemed to be coming from that way. We moved toward it, slowly at first, then faster. The closer we got, the louder and more urgent the sound became.

Then I saw something move between the pines. Not an animal. A woman—a white woman—standing not ten feet away. She was dressed in an old-fashioned riding costume and looked to be holding the reins of a bridle, but I didn't see any horse at the end of that bridle. As we got closer, the woman turned and glided farther into the trees.

Zora moved quickly and called out, "Wait!" But the woman was gone. Not just ahead of us and not out of reach, but nowhere at all.

I began to shiver.

Zora spun around, her eyes bright. "Did you see that?" she exclaimed.

My mouth was so dry I couldn't respond.

Without another word, Zora threw down the unwieldy rifle, grabbed Teddy by one arm, me by the other, and said, "Run!"

We raced along Teddy's marked trail, ignoring the stabs and scratches from branches and needles as we flew. I ran till my lungs felt like they would burst. We made it out of the forest in a fraction of the time it took us to make our way in. When we reached Mr. Polk's stable, we collapsed on a stiff mound of hay, gasping and welcoming the distance between us and the forest.

CHAPTER EIGHT

I couldn't stop shivering. Teddy noticed, but my
anger at him was the equal to my fear. I showed
him my back, grabbed my knees to warm myself,
and looked only at Zora.

Zora was busy trying to compose herself as well,
but the twin coiled springs of excitement and fear
wouldn't stop bouncing inside of her.

"OK, what was that all about?" Teddy asked,
panting.

"Did you see that?" Zora looked ready to pop.

"See what?" Teddy asked warily.

"The horse!" Zora shot back.

"I didn't *see* nothing. I *heard* something—an animal crying, I think—but it must have been still too far away for me to see it. I don't know what it is you think you saw."

"Are you blind? A big black shiny horse was standing not five feet in front of us, and you didn't see it?" She turned to me, afire with revelation. "I know you saw it, Carrie! Tell him!"

My scalp tingled and my heartbeat sped up again. Truthfully, I no longer knew what I had seen, even as I knew it was definitely not a horse. "Well . . ."

"Are you gonna stand there and tell me you didn't see nothing, either?"

"Of course she didn't," said Teddy. "There was nothing to see!"

Teddy speaking for me only stirred up the stew of my anger at him, and out of sheer annoyance, I immediately took Zora's side. "I did so see it! I saw it plain as day!" I was lying, but I *had* seen someone or something, so the lie rested on truth. That's what counted—that's what I told myself.

"But when we got closer," Zora continued, "it vanished. Into thin air! I tell you, that was no Moss Star, or any other of Mr. Polk's horses. That was no flesh-and-blood horse, period!"

Teddy rolled his eyes at us, and I had to keep myself from reaching over and pinching him hard.

"Zora," he said, "somewhere out there is a hurt and frightened animal for sure, but you grabbed us and took off running so fast that we're here instead of tending to the poor creature."

"Oh, so you were just running to keep us company. Is that it?" She put her hand on her hip for emphasis. "If Carrie and I hadn't been with you, you would have gone looking for that mysterious wounded animal in those spooky woods all on your own, is that it?"

Teddy at least was humble enough to shrug sheepishly at being called out. "Look, I ain't saying it wasn't spooky, hearing that sound and not seeing anything. I'm just saying there was no ghost horse."

"Then how do you account for what we saw, Mr. Scientist?"

"I don't have the faintest notion what y'all saw. Maybe it's this crazy weather and that spooky place playing tricks on our minds, is all."

"Is that what you think?" Zora huffed with frustration. "Honestly?" It usually pained me to see my two best friends at odds with each other, but after how Teddy had treated me earlier, I was in no mood to defend him.

"I'll bet you don't want to admit we saw a haint," I said a bit haughtily, "because the idea scares you too much."

Teddy looked at me steadily for a few seconds. "If y'all are going to gang up on me no matter what I say, then I'm calling it a day. I probably should have gone home a long time ago." And with that he got up, hung Mr. Polk's rope back on the wall, and started home. A few yards off, he turned and waved at us.

Neither of us moved a finger to wave back. If Teddy Baker could choose the pretense of common sense over what we saw with our own eyes, well, who needed Teddy Baker? But deep down I was secretly glad. If Teddy was at odds with Zora, too, she would be less likely to notice my anger at him.

Zora turned to me. "Do you believe in haints?" she asked.

I hesitated. My feelings about spirits were complicated. When my father went missing for such a long time, even though we didn't have hard proof of it, we knew he was dead. Still, I would wake up at dawn sometimes, sure I'd felt the touch of his rough palm on my cheek. Or I would be walking alone at dusk and the air would carry the soft sound of my name in his deep bass.

"Well," I answered Zora, "I think maybe a haint is something that's left over from when a person was living. Like the shadow of all their feelings still floating in the air."

"Mm," she said, nodding. "But I always think of haints as the spirits of people. You think animals can have haints, too? Why would a horse haunt a place?"

"Horses have souls, too, don't they? I reckon anything with a soul can have a haint."

Zora sprang to her feet and started pacing at top speed, looking so much like a small version of her father on the pulpit, full of fire and gospel.

"Carrie! A dead horse showed its spirit self to *us*, you and me. What business you think an animal haint can have with us?"

"Well..."

"Unless," she went on without pausing, "it was sending us a message!"

I didn't like the sound of that, but Zora was on a roll and there was no point in trying to stop her.

"I remember one time my mama talking about Mrs. Johnson calling on Old Lady Bronson after her husband died from a rattler bite. Mrs. Johnson told Old Lady Bronson that Mean done learn everything it knows from her husband, and that dying had barely slowed him down. She said his meanness was still pushing her clean wash into the mud, stopping her cow's milk, burning her chicken even as she stood there watching it fry, and a dozen other things to boot. Old Lady Bronson said there was only one way to knock the mean out of dead Mr. Johnson so he could rest, and that was to find out what he wanted. Old Lady Bronson had Mrs. Johnson sleep with a piece of coontie root under her pillow for a week. Sure enough, on the fifth night Mrs. Johnson said her husband came to her in a dream, talking about how he wanted to be buried with his pocket watch, which was hid in a little tin under their front step. Once she went out and buried the watch in his grave, Mrs. Johnson didn't have no more trouble out of him."

"What you saying, Zora? You think we need to sleep with coontie under our pillow?"

"No, silly! I'm saying that there's surely a soul in that plantation house that still ain't settled, and I'm not all that surprised. Something in Eatonville has been tingling my senses and pushing at my feet since last night. I'm saying that what we saw just now on Polk's land was likely just a taste of what's waking up—and I mean to be there 'fore it gets dressed!"

WESTIN

—•—

1855

CHAPTER NINE

The next morning Master Frederic's body was moved to the cool dark of the root cellar. Prisca did not leave her room, and we slaves went about our business.

Miss Caroline was wearing one of the dresses I had dyed black two weeks earlier in readiness for this occasion. For days after, my hands carried the dark stain of preparing for death.

Westin was set deep in Florida, and I could count on both hands the farms that could be reached in a day with a couple of fingers to spare. And although word had gone out yesterday, our closest neighbors were only arriving today to pay their respects.

I knew Rebecca would need me at the table. She called me in and I served the guests. They spoke softly to Miss Caroline and to Miss Alice, and Miss Caroline responded with quiet apologies for her tears.

Miss Alice stepped into the hall and asked me to bring Prisca. I knocked on her door, but she refused to answer. Even when I spoke in our old language, she would not respond.

I returned downstairs without her, and Miss Alice frowned at me but said nothing in front of the guests.

The next night Miss Alice once again asked me to summon Prisca, but this time she followed me up the stairs. She stepped in front of me and knocked on the locked door. "Prisca, honey, you've got to come down," she gently urged. "Mama is already suffering. Please don't add to her sorrow. Come down now and condole with the person who feels the loss as you do."

We heard a rustling from inside and slowly the door opened. Prisca stood before us dressed in black. Miss Alice smiled at her and took her arm. Prisca bowed her head and allowed herself to be led down. I followed behind, closing her back buttons as quickly as I could.

On my way back to the kitchen I saw Miss Caroline stand and embrace Prisca as she entered the dining room. Prisca melted into her arms and began weeping again.

At dinner they sat side by side, neither eating much. Miss Alice and Master George kept a light conversation going while their son, Timothy, finished everything on his plate.

When Miss Alice turned to engage her mother, Timothy sought his father's attention.

"Pa, up in an oak right at the tree line, what do you think I saw?"

Master George turned to his son, and though he didn't say anything, Timothy took that notice as a sign to continue. "It was a raccoon, but not just any raccoon. This was the biggest coon I ever saw — the biggest I'll bet anybody ever saw. It must have eaten five other raccoons to get that big. And what do you think I did?"

"What?" Master George asked, his interest piqued.

"Well, I took my time, I took aim, and I fired!"

Master George smiled then. "You got him?" he asked, looking pleased.

"No," said Timothy. "He moved at the last second, but I got the branch he was on, and boy did he go tumbling. He must have fallen twenty feet!" He was grinning, looking for his father's approval.

"Did you get him then?"

"What do you mean?"

"When he hit the ground," said his father. "After that twenty-foot fall. Did you get him then?"

Timothy looked confused. "Well, no. How could I? He was too fast. He just scrambled back in the brush. There wasn't time to reload."

Master George's smile sank. "Son, a man doesn't tell a story about his failure. No one wants to hear that story. Wait till you do something worth telling before you go bending people's ears." With that, he went back to his food.

Timothy's face darkened and his lip set tight. He had lost his father's fleeting attention. He looked over at his mother and grandmother, who were still in conversation, and Prisca's eyes were on her plate. He caught me looking at him then and gave me a nasty scowl.

I dropped my eyes immediately. I knew how quick he was to lash out at any slave who witnessed his humiliation.

At Christmas the year before, when Master Frederic and Miss Caroline had gifted Master George with a new stud, Master George turned to Horatio to break it in. It was a challenge even for Horatio, who could calm the most anxious horses. Nevertheless, he set out to do it as he did everything—with patience and persistence—and Master George was extremely pleased with his progress. To Master Frederic and Miss Caroline, he said, "The boy has the makings of a real trainer. He is doing a better job than I could do, and I know a thing or two about horses. You'll be hiring him out before long."

Timothy heard this, and I believe that his father's praise of a slave was an insult to him, a sharp wound.

Burning to prove himself a horseman the equal to his father—and certainly better than a slave— Timothy took the new steed into the corral. As soon as the boy got in the saddle, the animal threw him with such force that in landing he broke his large toe. Master George chided Timothy about the incident for as long as he needed a crutch afterward. Timothy used that crutch not only for walking, but to strike out at Horatio whenever he found himself alone with him. Openly hitting Horatio would have betrayed his jealousy, so his attacks on Horatio were furtive, quick, and painful. Horatio never said a word, not even when I touched those wounds as we sat reading from the books I stole from Prisca's room. He would push my hand away, drawing my attention to the lesson.

My thoughts were abruptly brought back to the present when Prisca spilled her wine. I rushed to stop the spread of its stain on the tablecloth.

Master George took this as a signal to end supper, asking everyone to join him in the library. I moved to clear the dishes so I could pull the tablecloth for soaking, but George turned to me and said, "Leave this, Lucia. Our conversation includes you."

My mouth went dry and my stomach tightened, and I stiffly followed the others to the parlor.

I stood by the door while everyone else took their places, Master George next to Miss Caroline, Miss Alice next to Timothy, Prisca by herself. Master George began without preamble. "Alice and I have decided to leave Saint Augustine and move here."

"What?" Timothy stood. "No!"

"Do not question your father, Timothy," Miss Alice said in a firm tone that suggested she had anticipated this protest.

"But I don't want to leave Saint Augustine! I have no friends here!"

"Timothy!" Master George's voice resounded against the dark wood panels. "We all have to make sacrifices. Your mother and I are also leaving those whose company we care for so that we may see your grandmother through this time of mourning. I am leaving my law practice to run the farm."

I stood perfectly still, silent as the drapes, but watchful as an owl. I had often suspected Master George wanted Westin, and now the opportunity was presenting itself.

Unlike Prisca's father, who considered himself above the daily disciplining of slaves, Master George seemed enlivened by the task. Since his arrival eight weeks ago, Master George had given Mr. Krowse free rein, something Master Frederic had never done. "Do what you must, Krowse. The ends justify the means." For the field slaves, this meant more lashes for more infractions, and smaller rations for longer days. There would be heartache when they heard this news.

Sullen, Timothy pointed at Prisca and asked, "What about her? What does she have to sacrifice?"

Prisca almost smiled. "What do I have left to sacrifice? I've lost my mother and my father. I have nothing else." She turned to Miss Caroline, who nodded solemnly.

"It's true. Your father did not leave you anything."

Prisca blinked. I think she had not until that

moment given a single thought to her material needs, but the words *did not leave you anything* gave her a notion that there might have been something for her father to leave her. But he had not. Her mouth formed a small O.

Miss Caroline continued, "Of course I will care for you until you marry." She paused, perhaps to let her words find purchase in Prisca's mind. Prisca blinked slowly but did not move. "I am not a mercenary person. If I were, I would not have married your father. But between your upkeep and Alice and George's removal from Saint Augustine, I'm going to need for your father to now, belatedly, adhere to the terms of our marriage contract."

Prisca's eyes widened. "Marriage contract? What do you mean?"

"I am having George and Alice take Lucia to Saint Augustine. She will be sold there, and the proceeds used to support the farm."

I felt pressure behind my eyes, and my hands turned to ice in the hot room.

Prisca was on her feet. "No! Lucia will not be sold!" She looked at me. "She's mine! She's always been mine! I would never sell her!"

Miss Caroline looked pained. "Prisca, I know this comes at a terrible time, but I don't have a choice. It is what's best for the family. If you listen to reason you'll see . . ."

"I will not! That's not reason, selling Lucia. That's the opposite of reason!"

I tried to look at the faces in the room, but I could not make my eyes see them clearly. All I heard were the words *She will be sold.*

"Prisca, dear, I implore you," Miss Caroline continued. "You yourself just acknowledged it. You said so yourself—you have nothing!"

"Yes, but not Lucia! I didn't mean Lucia! My father would never have consented to sell her!"

Sweat pooled under my arms. Prisca was defending me—not because I was a person and should not be sold, but because I was her property and could not be taken from her.

Miss Caroline looked stricken. "It was never a question of consent. He brought her to the marriage; he promised a bar of gold and the sale of a girl slave. When you arrived and he saw how upset you were at . . . how isolating the farm can be, he wanted to wait. He didn't want you to be lonely. He asked if we could hold off selling her for as long as the gold lasted, and I, against my instincts but because I loved him and because I saw how unhappy you were, I said yes. I said yes, but now your father is gone and the gold is gone, and I have no choice."

Prisca shook her head violently. "No. I refuse to believe it. My father would never allow this."

Miss Caroline shook her head and began to rise from her seat, but Master George stood first and said, "I'll get it, Mother Caroline."

He went to the corner desk where Miss Caroline always sat to do the accounts, and from a drawer he drew a rolled scroll tied with a ribbon. He slid off the ribbon and unrolled the parchment as he approached Prisca. "It's the marriage contract. Read the fourth paragraph from the top: 'In consideration of . . .' Right here."

Prisca held the stiff document open with one hand at the top and one hand at the bottom. "'In consideration of the above,'" she read aloud, "'the Husband agrees to bring his extensive library, a bar of pure gold weighing not less than four hundred troy ounces, and a girl slave to be sold upon arrival. . . .'" Prisca's voice trailed off and she lowered the contract. My stomach churned.

Master George put a hand on Prisca's shoulder. "You must understand how distasteful this is to all of us." Miss Caroline and Miss Alice murmured their assent. "But we have to think about the good of the whole family, and it would be unconscionable to indulge one at the expense of the others."

Prisca's voice was hollow. "Is there no money left at all?"

George looked uncomfortable at the question. "The fact is that we need ready money to remove from Saint Augustine to here. Lucia has learned to be a good servant. She has manners and a pleasing appearance, and she will bring a fine price in a port city. Mother Caroline has brought up the matter now because I will leave for Saint Augustine after your father's funeral, sell Lucia at the market there, and then undertake all the other measures we have discussed."

Prisca went to kneel before Miss Caroline. "Caroline, please, I beg of you. Please don't sell Lucia. Please."

My body was on fire. The whole conversation revolved around me and I could no more speak for myself than could the chair beside me.

Miss Caroline stroked Prisca's head, even as she looked imploringly at her son-in-law and daughter.

George spoke. "The decision has been made. The decision is final. The girl will be sold."

Prisca stood up and rushed over to me. "Never. Never. Never," she said, grabbed my wrist, and pulled me out of the parlor, up the stairs, and into her room.

I sat with my back against the wall and hugged my knees to my chest. A storm was coming, and there was no shelter for me.

Prisca sank to her knees, covered her face, and sobbed. "We are undone. We have lost everything! All that could be taken from us is gone. My father is dead and now we are at the mercy of these heartless people!"

I could only stare at her. I was full of so many feelings: anger that even she believed I could be owned—that any person could be owned; despair that in only a few days' time I would be ripped from everything and everyone I knew; horror at the thought of what awaited me at the hands of a new owner. All those feelings I had spent three years stifling wanted to come roaring out of me, and it took all my will to keep them in check.

I waited until the tempest of her tears subsided

before I spoke. "I was brought here three years ago with no say in the matter. In that time I have been shown no mercy."

Prisca's eyes met mine and she squinted slightly, as if emerging from a fog. "Except by me!" she proclaimed. "I've done everything possible to lighten your burden!"

I dropped my eyes. I could not lie without erasing myself, and I could not tell the truth without erasing her. I wanted to tell her, *No. You are not an exception. As long as there are slaves, the free benefit. If it were not for slavery, we would all be merely human. It's our slavery that makes you free.*

She pressed on. "I will not let them take you! I won't!"

I took her hand, hoping that would make her hear my actual words. "Prisca, there is nothing you can do for me."

She recoiled and started weeping again.

Though my words were true, they did not bring me satisfaction. To cause her pain would be to seek revenge for something that lay beyond what either of us could control.

I pressed my brow to my knees and tried to still

my terror. *To be sold.* The words kept echoing in my head. I was no more than a bale of hay, a pallet of wood, a sow for slaughter. I was nothing, and if you are nothing, anything can be done to you. I burned with fear, sorrow, humiliation, and helplessness. And not one of Prisca's tears could extinguish that fire.

CHAPTER TEN

Barely half an hour had passed when there was a knock at the door. Prisca stood stiffly, wiped her eyes with her sleeve, and answered it.

On the other side of the door stood Miss Caroline. She spoke softly. "Prisca, I know it is grief that makes your behavior untoward. But this behavior . . . it makes everything so much harder. Please send Lucia out now and show me that you are still the good, sensible girl I know you to be. Things can easily be made right between us."

Prisca's eyes were wild. "*Made right?* If you take Lucia, I promise you nothing will ever be right between us again!"

Miss Caroline took Prisca's words like a blow. She stepped aside, revealing the presence of Master George and Mr. Krowse.

There was no more talking. Mr. Krowse pushed past Prisca and came over to me. He reached down and yanked me up by the wrists as if I weighed no more than a little sack of flour. Before I was even fully standing, he dragged me from the room.

Prisca lunged at Mr. Krowse and began to beat him with her fists. Startled, Master George grabbed her from behind. She started to scream, all the while reaching for me and struggling to free herself from Master George's grip. Mr. Krowse pulled me toward the stairs. "Step lively," he said, "unless you want to go down headfirst."

As he continued to yank me along, fear finally took over from shock and I began to struggle.

I was near the bottom of the stairs, while Prisca was still at the top, trying to break free of Master George's grip. Miss Caroline was nowhere to be seen.

I stopped short to look back at Prisca, which took Mr. Krowse by surprise. His foot missed the next landing and he stumbled, letting go of my hand. I tried to bolt back up the stairs toward Prisca, but he was too quick for me. He recovered his balance, grabbed me, and threw me down the remaining three steps.

I lay on the floor at the foot of the stairs, choking for breath. Then I saw it: his hand reaching for the whip that was always holstered to his belt. The first time I saw it I marveled at how small it was, how unimposing: a slim wooden handle the length of a man's hand, a skinny cowhide braid the length of an arm, a tiny lozenge of leather at the very end. But I had seen him use it at least a dozen times. I knew the lozenge held a ball of lead, and I had seen the damage that modest object could do.

It arced in the air and then lightning tore across my back. In that instant I flew out of myself, above myself, floated weightlessly above my empty body, watching as he delivered two more punishing lashes. And as I floated over the body that had no self in it, I saw again every whipping I had witnessed at Westin. In all my imaginings, I had underestimated the agony.

Sibby had run the previous summer, and she was gone long enough that we had come to think of her as free — free or dead. Even the paddyrollers — white men who organized themselves into patrols on the lookout for slaves unaccompanied by a master, and who chased runaways for reward money—tired of searching for her.

I remember Master Frederic and Miss Caroline shaking their heads over dinner, wondering aloud how a slow-headed girl of fifteen could possibly run away with no help.

But Mr. Krowse, relentless in his pursuit, thought to question the Seminoles by Lake Apopka. Though he couldn't bribe them to reveal that a black girl with a burn scar on her arm was among them, he had better luck with a white trader who dealt with them, and her hiding place was revealed. Warned by the Seminoles, she gained a few hours on Mr. Krowse and his hunting party. She ran into the swamps, managing to avoid the noses of the dogs. Three men pursued her for six days before she gave herself up, brought down by hunger and fever. They brought her back to Westin in chains.

Mr. Krowse ordered all the slaves on the farm to watch him whip Sibby. We knew it would be terrible. Twenty lashes? Forty? When Mr. Krowse told us that anyone who interfered would get the same, Leopold, larger than everyone else on the plantation at well over six feet tall, shook his head bitterly and whispered, "Fifty lashes." Mr. Krowse tied Sibby to the gatepost, but the fever was cresting in her body and she no longer had the strength to stand, so he tied her at the waist against the trunk of a camphor tree to keep her from falling. He then delivered the first lash.

Sibby woke from the delirium of her fever and screamed, her single cry a hundred times more penetrating than a pig's during slaughter. Then she was silent. By the seventh lash, Sibby fell, unconscious, against the ropes.

Mr. Krowse cursed her. He kicked her limp body. He spat on the ground and threatened us with worse if we ever tried to run. Finally he turned and walked away. Leopold and Samuel undid the ropes that held Sibby's fevered body, and Samuel carried her to the shack she had once shared with Abeline. Samuel was Rebecca's younger brother, and although he was shy, we all knew he had been sweet on Sibby for a good long time. His arms were trembling as he laid her down on the straw pallet. I put my hand on his back to steady him. Sibby was still breathing, but it came from her in broken gasps. Rebecca, who had silently entered behind me, shook her head, her eyes locked on Samuel's grieving face.

I sat with Sibby that night, bathing her forehead with cool water and waving a burlap sack to keep the flies away. When she took her last breath, I stopped and placed my hand on her still chest and felt the fever subside under my hand. I recalled Sibby laughing, dancing with Samuel while Abeline sang a song about the devil and beauty. I recalled her face the last day I saw her before she ran and how it revealed nothing about her plans, how not even Samuel knew. And I recalled the death of Mama Sezelle's brother, how she had covered him with cloth and lit a candle at his head and feet, how the old women gathered to release his soul. Who would release Sibby's soul?

I gathered what I could find: a sheet, with almost as many holes as patches, and a small stub of a candle. I lit the candle and I spoke what I could remember of Mama Sezelle's words. Three years without hearing the cadence of our island talk, the words no longer came easily, but I tried. I tried to set Sibby free.

When Rebecca entered the cabin she caught her breath to see Sibby laid out, and she sat down heavily beside me. She spoke, but it was more to herself than to me. "Travel in any direction, you're still nowhere. This land is so wild, and we're so, so far from anything: you escape, they catch you. Our lives ain't nothing but a hunt to them. If I tell Samuel to run, this is how he'll come back to me."

I took her hand and held it tight. The secret we all

shared, the one every white person wanted to beat out of us, was the burning desire to run. Freedom.

The next day Prisca had asked me what I knew about the slave who ran, so I told her Sibby's story. Horrified by the details, Prisca had cried, "If only she hadn't run. If she hadn't run, she would still be alive!" Then she closed herself in the library.

A wave of rage had crashed over me. Prisca was a girl whom Mama Sezelle had cared for with tender hands, who had lain under lime trees with me and counted eggs in the nests of bobo birds. That same girl had put away the pain of Sibby's death by simply closing a door, and when she did, my heart broke.

But this time was different. This time the girl they were whipping belonged to Prisca. She was running down the steps toward me and screaming, "Stop it! Stop it! George, make him stop! Please, George! For the love of God!"

Master George yelled down the stairs, "Krowse! Do not reduce her value!"

Prisca began cursing in our island language. She cursed Master George and Krowse.

I wondered how she could cry when I felt numb, but when she knelt on the floor and took me into her arms, my body woke up and the iron-hot burn of the lashes made me whimper.

Rebecca appeared in the doorway, her neck beading perspiration, her eyes bright with fear. Master George looked at her and pointed to me. "Take her to the cabins."

Rebecca walked toward us steadily. When she reached us, I pushed Prisca away and grabbed Rebecca with all my strength, desperate to escape the pain in my body.

Prisca looked hurt as I clung to Rebecca. Then she turned on Master George, hissing like a barn cat. "I hate you!"

Master George retorted, "Oh, no, Prisca. Oh, no. Don't pretend this is *my* handiwork. You have yourself to thank. Treating her like an equal, acting like she's one of us, carrying on like a spoiled child when we treat her like what she is, almost ruining her for good use. Slaves are not people, Prisca, and they are not pets. They are property, and not *your* property. They do not belong to you. They are the property of this plantation."

Prisca glared at him. "If you are my people, then I am no longer one of you."

CHAPTER ELEVEN

I was curled in a ball on the packed-earth floor of Rebecca's cabin, shivering. My teeth were chattering so hard I might have bit off my tongue. Rebecca spoke slowly and quietly to me, as if I were a small child. My body felt like a cold metal shell, and I was rattling around inside, bumping up against its walls. Rebecca kept talking quietly. Finally, her words broke through. "Come, child, let me tend to the wounds. Shh, child. Come, it's OK now."

Finally I got my mouth to work, and I said "No" as loudly as I could, as long as I could, until I grew weary. Then I just breathed, jagged breaths. I could feel Rebecca's hand stroking my head, her words falling softly on my hair.

Then Rebecca was helping me to sit upright. She was gently undoing the top of my smock, her words still falling softly around me.

"Angry snakes," she said, kneeling behind me, examining my back. "That's what you got. Three angry snakes."

I could feel two of them writhing in fire on my back. One stretched from my back all the way around to my chest and under my heart, searing me like a hot coal. Rebecca dabbed it with a cool, wet cloth.

"You ain't 'customed to the lash. But for so few, they won't let you lie in." She spoke low. "I'll let the wounds cool tonight and bandage you up tight in the morning."

I nodded. The measurement of fitness to work against the damage of the lash was so common that they had a formula for it, a special calculus.

I moaned, and mumbled, "I saw Leopold take fifteen and work the field the next day." A wave of anger at my own weakness washed over me.

Rebecca shook her head. "The lash hits everyone different. Take three of you to make Leopold, another lifetime of hard work to do what he do."

"They're going to sell me!" I spit. The accent of my island tongue thickened my words. Then my rage fled as fast as it came, leaving a voice so small I could hardly hear it. "They're going to sell me," I whispered.

Rebecca grunted. She pulled me to her, my head in her lap, and stroked my hair again. "You hold tight to yourself. A lot of us been sold away, and we're still alive."

The door hinge groaned and we both looked up. Horatio stepped into the cabin, his brow creased with worry. He sat down beside us and took my hand.

Rebecca nodded to him. "They gonna sell her," she said.

His grip on my hand tightened, and after several minutes he spoke. "My first master, he sold me away from my mama when I was five. Sometimes I wake up and see Mama. I see her running after that trader's cart, calling my name. My new master, he hauled wood, but I was so small I couldn't pull the loads. He lost me in a card game. The man that won me, he tied me to the wall of his barn and burned his mark into my back with a glowing poker. He sold me five months later. Six masters owned me by the time Miss Caroline's first husband bought me. I learned that if I could keep my body alive I could live through most anything." He searched my eyes, trying to see how his words had landed inside me.

"I hate them," I answered. "I hate them all."

He caressed my hand. "These white folks pay for what they do. They just don't know it. They pay with a little bit of their soul every time they put their boot on us. Ain't no man nor woman can bring another soul low without losing they own soul. They may not think they lost, but they are."

His patient words only angered me more. "I *know* their souls are already dead. But their bodies still sleep in soft beds in big houses, wear fine clothes, and eat good food. Their fine boots still get to kick us down and kick us again while we're down. They still sell us like barnyard animals, breaking our hearts as if we had none, when it's they who have no hearts. I hate them!"

"You can do that," he said. "You can hate, but hate too hard and it'll steal the memory of what you love. Hate long enough, and you won't feel nothing for no one."

I wept to hear his words because they held my truth. My hate felt like a poison in me, and it altered nothing about our lives.

Hot tears of frustration ran down my face. Horatio leaned close to me. "No matter where they take you, you will always live in my mind, just like the words you taught me to read."

I bawled to hear those words, and Rebecca wept, too, as she stroked my hair, saying over and over, "It's gonna be all right. You gonna live through this pain. You gonna survive."

Some while later Horatio left, and Rebecca, after easing me, facedown, onto my pallet, extinguished the one candle with a sharp exhale.

The next morning I opened my eyes to see Rebecca already up. She had boiled rags the night before, and now she gently laid them, cool with the morning dew, on my wounds, then carefully wound a broad strip of muslin around my torso. We didn't say a word.

All day I could feel the cloth scraping my back like a sea of razors. In the cookhouse I would arch my back, the cloth pulling at every turn, but I clenched my teeth, not willing to give them the satisfaction of having bowed me, and I worked as I always had.

When I served breakfast, Master George barely glanced my way. I had been dealt with and no longer merited a thought. Prisca could not bring herself to look at me at all, but her cheeks flamed red.

Afternoon brought more neighbors from farther

afield to condole. For two of the families who came, it was a journey of at least four hours on rough roads. One family came from the area they called Fort Maitland, although the fort was long gone. Their barn had burned down eight months before, and Master Frederic had loaned them Jeremiah and Leopold, able carpenters both, to help them rebuild it. During the rebuilding and after, Prisca struck up a friendship with their son, Jude. Given that Jude would inherit his father's lumber mill, it was a friendship that did not go unremarked upon by Miss Alice.

As the afternoon wore on, Rebecca sent me to fetch buttermilk from the root cellar, and on my way back I saw Prisca walking quickly toward the porch. Behind her by at least twenty feet was Jude. His hands were stuffed in his pockets and he kicked at high grass. He called her name and she stopped. He ran to her and took her hands, speaking urgently. She shook her head, pried her hands from his, and ran back to the house. Master Jude watched her go but did not follow.

The guests had an early supper. Miss Caroline had used her best china, and Rebecca and I then washed and dried every single piece of fragile porcelain. A broken cup would be met with a smack or worse.

Outside I gazed up at the bright stars and thought about everything I had lost and would lose. I thought of Mama Sezelle. Was she looking at the same stars now? Were we truly bound by her words over a small wooden bowl so long ago? I had begun to doubt the power of the island women. If their magic was real, why could it not save me now?

As I neared the barn, someone reached out and clasped my shoulder from behind. I almost screamed with fright, but it was only Prisca, pale and trembling in her mourning dress.

She pulled me behind a cypress tree and spoke intensely. "I spoke with Jude this afternoon, but it is useless."

I brushed her hand from my arm. "Prisca, I am too tired to understand what you are saying." All I wanted was to lie down on my pallet in Rebecca's cabin.

She took a deep breath. "I had thought Jude might rescue us. I offered him my hand in marriage."

I gasped. I could not help it. "You want to marry . . . ?"

"Yes, and he says he wants to marry me but not

until he gets his inheritance, which is years from now—three years—and we cannot wait."

"You have plenty of time to marry."

"Not me and Jude. Me and you. Do you think I don't understand what coming here has meant? Had he married me, I could have bought you! I could have moved us *both* from this place. Don't you see?"

Slowly I did.

EATONVILLE

1903

CHAPTER TWELVE

I helped Zora and Sarah put dinner on the table. Since Zora hadn't brought back the nails until late in the day, Lucy Hurston had let John escape to his favorite fishing hole after all. And we were now about to feast on the bigmouth bass he caught. There were buttermilk biscuits and swamp cabbage and glasses of cool molasses water. Everything looked and smelled as good as food could, but I didn't have much appetite. We all sat down and joined hands, and Mr. Hurston gave the blessing.

"Precious Lord, for these gifts, we thank you. Amen." Then he sat down and bit into a biscuit. We gaped at each other, stunned at the speed and brevity of the muttered words. We ventured our tentative "Amens."

Normally he presided over dinner the way he did over his pulpit, with a booming mini-sermon, then holding forth on the day's events, reviewing his children's deeds and misdeeds, and proclaiming how the world should work. His God-given power of speech seemed to have failed him this evening. There was only the sound of forks against plates, small slurping noises from Everett, and the rustling of hands reaching. Everyone was uneasy. I felt the way I do when the chickens hide and my mama lifts her head and says she smells a hurricane coming. His quiet muted even Zora.

Zora was watching her mama, who was watching Mr. Hurston, the food on her plate untouched.

It was Sarah who spoke first. "Daddy, you think this storm's gonna break soon?"

Mr. Hurston put down his fork and looked at his favorite daughter. His eyes softened. "Let's hope the storm changes course before it gets to us. That's what I'm praying on."

Sarah nodded and fell back into silence. Zora's older brothers swapped a serious look. This night even they didn't make noise, argue, or snatch biscuits.

After dinner, while Zora and I started silently clearing the dishes, there was a knock on the door. Mr. Hurston opened it and let in Joe Clarke.

Zora ran up to him. "Mr. Clarke, what brings you to our place tonight?"

"Why, to see my favorite Eatonville resident, of course!" He smiled, and Zora grinned.

A second knock a moment later brought the Baker men — Mr. Baker, Micah, and Jake. At that point, Zora and I knew nobody was paying a social call. Something serious was happening, and the men of the town were gathering.

Mr. Hurston looked at Sarah, Cliff, Ben, Everett, Zora, and me and spoke sternly. "Y'all go on up to bed, hear? We got town business to discuss, and it don't concern children." Since John and Dick were standing behind him, it obviously did concern at least two of his children, but we knew enough not to press the point.

Sarah gathered a wriggling Everett into her arms and began shooing us to our rooms. Zora, one step ahead of her father, grabbed my dress and pulled me to the side. We ducked into her parents' bedroom, right off the main room where the men were gathering. She closed the door all the way except for a crack and together we peered through. Lucy Hurston had taken her regular seat by the unlit fireplace and took up her darning. More knocks, and more of Eatonville's men filled the room.

Some fifteen minutes later things got underway. As mayor, Joe Clarke opened the meeting and laid out the problem at hand.

"Here's the situation. This morning two white men came 'round to see me: a land agent from Winter Park and a man from Jacksonville, name of Peterson. They claim that old Polk's land was never legally abandoned, so it was illegal to join it in parcel with the land sold to Eatonville. They said I needed to dispossess Polk and they would ride out with me to make sure I did."

That set off an explosion of exclamations. "Say what, now?" "Oh, no!" "I don't believe it!" "Nuh-uh!"

Mr. Clarke raised his hand for quiet. "I showed them our charter and the deed to the parcel of the whole town. I showed them the part where it says the land Polk's on now was declared legally abandoned in 1870 and made part of Eatonville in 1887. I showed them the record of Polk's purchase of the land in that same year."

More murmurs, and Mr. Clarke held up his hand.

"Hang on, men, I ain't finished. The land agent represents Peterson, and he says the man's claim on the land had been ignored after the war. He says that his client has come to reclaim the land that is rightfully his, and that he bears the deed to it."

Chester Cools stood up. "Did he show it to you? Did he show you the deed?"

Mr. Clarke scowled. "We know darn well he doesn't have one, Chester."

Mr. Cools looked embarrassed. "Well, I was just giving you the opportunity to say so. That's a mighty important detail on such a significant matter." He looked around the room. "Significant!"

Zora elbowed me. She loved the way folks whose speech was plain as gray wool in normal times liked to trot out their biggest words on special occasions, as if they had been saving them up and didn't want to waste them on everyday things. We agreed that her father was king of the fifty-cent words, but there were a lot of dukes and earls and counts in the kingdom of Eatonville, too!

This was met by even more agitated murmuring.

"It is significant, yes," Mr. Clarke continued, "but this Peterson says he did present his deed to the county clerk up in Sanford, and the clerk raised no

objection to his legal attempts to reclaim the land."
More murmuring, and Mr. Clarke spoke still louder.
"Peterson says his call this morning was his 'legal
attempt at redress.' That's what he calls it. Now, I
deny his claim . . ."

"Of course you do!"

"I denied his claim, telling him if he wants to dispute my decision, he'll have to file a formal complaint
at the courthouse in—"

Mr. Hurston was on his feet. "Now, why you do
that, Joe, tell him he could dispute it? Why you go
do that?"

"John, as a marshal I'm a sworn officer of the law,
and it's my duty to—"

"No, no. No, it ain't, Joe. I beg to differ. Your
duty is to protect and defend the people of this town,
not to succor the enemy!"

"John, let me finish what I—"

"No, no, you let *me* finish. I was born into slavery,
like most of us here. I was a slave the first two years
of my life, and I'll be damned if I ever be one again!
Taking land from one of us is the same as all of us
having no land at all. They take our land once, what's
to stop them from taking it again?"

"It's a fact," called out Mr. Edges. "Ain't no law bestowed with the purpose of protecting any man but the white man." Zora and I looked at each other with surprise. It was the most animated we had ever seen or heard Mr. Edges in our lives.

Teddy's father stood. Mr. Baker wasn't a member of the dictionary club, but folks listened to him. "Bertram's right, Joe. There's nothing white folks won't do when colored folks have something they want."

Mr. Clarke looked weary, but his voice was strong. "I hear what you men are saying, but when I became the marshal of Lake Maitland in 1885 I bided my time. I waited. And, when I needed to, I groveled." We heard the whole room catch its breath at that word. "I did, because always, in the back of my mind, there was the dream—that one day I would found a town for colored people, run by colored people. And my dream for that town was everything this country had denied us—a place where we could be free, where we could govern ourselves, and where the law that makes the dream of democracy real for white folks would make it real for us, too."

We could make out a few low "Amens" and a couple of "That's rights."

"I made my dream come to pass. Y'all are standing on my dream made flesh."

The room fell deathly silent.

"Now, I need to tell you something else: when we choose against the law, we're choosing against our own dream — the dream of what's fair and civil and decent. We're choosing to side with the logic of the mob, with the worst this country is, and the worst it can dole out. And we know what white folks do when colored men take up arms — ain't no mystery around that. We've got to try to rebuild this country with its own building blocks, and that means we need to keep trying the law. If we don't have the courage and the patience to do that, we'll trade blood for blood, clear through to our great-grandchildren."

Mr. Hurston nodded. "I hear you, Joe, and I respect what you say. We got to render unto Caesar the things which are Caesar's, but what does Caesar render unto us? The white man is our Caesar, and he takes from us, all right, but he does not give to us, and he does not protect us from injustice. Think about the Seminole. What good the law do him? We all residing — white and colored both — on Seminole land. So why we think we can make the law protect us any more than it did the Seminole?"

Micah and Jake Baker nodded vigorously in agreement, until their father raised an eyebrow in their direction.

"What you say is true, John," said Mr. Clarke. "We've done everything legal through and through, but what I saw in that man's eyes today reminded me of things I want to forget."

No one said a word, but I believed I could hear the beating of every heart under that roof.

It was Mrs. Hurston who broke the silence. "Why don't you say it, Joe?" Her sewing had fallen to the floor and she was leaning forward, her face tight as a drum. "You think he's going to gather men, don't you?"

Joe Clarke exhaled slowly. "That's why I called this meeting, Lucy. I'm sorry you have to hear this, but my old neighbor Fred Callett rode down from Lake Maitland this afternoon to tell me that while he was making a delivery at the back of a pharmacy up there, a white-haired white man was riling up a bunch of boys about 'renegade nigras down in Eatonville.'" He let that sink in. "In fifteen years this town has never had so much as a whiff of the abomination this state is notorious for, but I'm afraid the coming days may change that."

"What we gonna do, Joe?" That was Mr. Eddie Jackson, a small nutmeg-colored man who lived with his sister and together sewed half the work clothes white Lake Maitland wore.

Joe looked grim. "I'm going to use the law. I will bring a formal letter to the mayor and the sheriff of Lake Maitland tomorrow and ask them to sit down and talk. Peterson don't care a fig for Eatonville law, but, if they side with us, Lake Maitland law is the white man's law, and he's bound to respect that, like it or not."

Mr. Hurston was not so easily pacified. "I say we pull tight and keep our guns ready." This suggestion was met with more enthusiasm than Joe's plan.

"I'm curious about one thing." This was Doc Brazzle, who up until then had been smoking his pipe in silence. "What does Polk have to say about this? Why isn't he here? Do we know for a fact that he wants to keep all that land? Maybe he could work out a compromise with these people? He doesn't use but a fraction of it, and it's worthless for growing anyway—

Mr. Slayton chimed in. "Yes, why don't he tell us himself? I would deeply love to hear that!"

This brought the first nervous laughter of the night.

"Very funny, Luke," said Mr. Clarke. "Very funny. Fact is, I already been to see old Polk. I found him with his arm bandaged up. As far as I could tell, he had already given those men his answer, and they were not able to work out a *compromise*, as Doc so eloquently put it."

"But, Joe" — Mr. Hurston wasn't standing and he wasn't puffed up or loud, but his jaw was set hard — "if they do gather men . . . if they do come for Polk . . . ?"

Mr. Clarke laid a hand on the pistol that always dangled from his belt. "If they gather men, if they come for Polk . . . then every man in this town will arm himself and head for Polk's, and we will defend our own. And God save Eatonville."

Those were the words nobody wanted to hear, yet everybody was waiting for. With nothing else to do or say, the men left and made their way home.

Joe Clarke was the last to leave, but stood by the door with Zora's parents for another moment.

"The past is coming for us, isn't it?" Mrs. Hurston asked. "A lynch mob is coming here as surely as I saw them come to Notasulga, back in Alabama. White men with lynching ropes will hang us from trees here as easy as they did in Alabama. We were foolish to think there could ever be a safe place, that we could ever get away."

"Eatonville ain't Alabama," said Joe Clarke. "It ain't Mississippi, and it ain't any place else in the rest of Florida. We built this place to make a fresh start, and as long as I draw breath I will protect Eatonville and every one of her residents. They may come, but Eatonville ain't gonna go easy."

In an equally somber tone, Mr. Hurston added, "For all we cleared this land, and built it up, and invested every cent we had to make this our Eden, white folks can turn it into hell on earth in one day."

Joe Clarke squeezed Lucy Hurston's hand and walked into the night.

Zora sat back, eyes shining. "Mr. Polk was stabbed by that white man we saw at Joe Clarke's store!" she whispered.

I was beginning to see the shape of something bigger than the secret Zora and I thought we were keeping: we held no secret at all. Everything we knew was just a tiny detail of a much larger picture, whose ugliness was growing clearer as the image revealed itself.

"What are we gonna do?" I whispered back.

Zora was thinking so hard that it pulled her face in twenty different directions. "Mr. Polk is protecting that land. That land, with the husk of a plantation on it, is worth more to him than his life. It means enough to him to risk all of Eatonville. Why? There has to be a reason."

"Like your daddy said, if they take land from one person, they can take it from everybody."

"I know that already," she snapped, drumming her fingers on her leg. "But that don't explain why it means so much to *him*. He's not gonna tell us anything, but there is one person who knows as much of the truth as there is to speak of."

I knew who she meant before she even said the name, and I really wished I didn't.

"Mm-hm. Old Lady Bronson. Whatever Mr. Polk is hiding, she has a good idea what it is. If she tells us, maybe — just maybe — we can help Daddy and Joe Clarke hold this thing off. If we do nothing, we're just a pile of sticks waiting for a match."

I guessed Zora was as scared as I was, but nothing could stop her from trying to save the people and the town she loved. It was like Mr. Hurston said: Eatonville was us and we were Eatonville.

I peered out into the main room to see Lucy Hurston take her husband's arm and him follow her into the kitchen, bending over her small frame and listening intently to her quiet words. Seeing our escape route cleared, we hightailed it up to Zora's room.

When we opened the door, there sat Sarah, wide-awake as a barn owl, eyes glinting in the candlelight, and Everett sound asleep next to her. But instead of chastising us or threatening to tattle, she was somber as the night.

"Zora," she whispered. "Did you find out what's going on?"

Zora sat down beside her. "White men want to take Mr. Polk's land. Mama thinks they might ride against Eatonville to do it."

Sarah shivered. "Do Daddy and Joe Clarke think they can stop them?"

"I don't know. They mean to try, but I don't know." Zora's words, so empty of hope, hung in the room. Sarah nodded but said nothing else. Zora got up, and Sarah, rather than moving Everett to his own bed, tucked herself in next to him.

I slipped out of my dress and crawled under the rough sheets. A minute later Zora did the same.

Sarah broke the silence, her voice fierce in the dark. "I'm glad you listened, Zora. Part of me wishes I didn't know, but not knowing would be worse."

In that moment I saw that no matter how many superficial differences Sarah and Zora had, a cable of sameness, strong as steel, ran through the sisters. There was Lucy Hurston in Sarah, too.

Dry lightning flashed outside, illuminating the room with a suddenness that threw everything into stark relief. It was the same with my understanding of tonight. I thought I knew everything about Eatonville, but as the lightning of race hate lit up our town, I saw how vulnerable we really were. No matter how clear our town borders seemed to me, they could be disregarded at any moment by white men who sought to hurt us.

WESTIN

1855

CHAPTER THIRTEEN

The next day was long. I spent from sunup till late afternoon in the washhouse. The humidity kept my back from drying, and the open sores wept through the bandages and the back of my shift.

My first respite came when Rebecca stuck her head in to say that Master George wanted me to serve at the dinner table. She caught sight of the back of my shift. "I'll fix you up before you go," she said. "Won't give him the satisfaction."

It was the first time seeing Prisca since our strange meeting the night before. Clearing the plates, I glimpsed an uneasy watchfulness on Master George's face. The moment I reached his plate, he addressed his son.

"Timothy, you told me a troubling story last night. I would like you to repeat it now."

Timothy flushed, but his eyes were bright.

He looked across the table at Prisca and announced, "Prisca wants Jude to marry her. She wants him to marry her so she can leave Westin and take Lucia with her. I heard her say so. *She* asked Jude to marry *her!*"

Miss Caroline put down her spoon and gaped at Prisca. "Is this true? Did you offer yourself in marriage? To young Jude?"

Prisca stared at Timothy, her eyes blazing. "The child has no idea what he's saying!"

Timothy bridled at the insult. "I'm no child—I'm fourteen! I know what I heard!"

"I believe the boy," Master George returned quietly. "Prisca, why would you do such a shameful thing?"

Prisca stared at George and uttered not one word.

"Prisca, dearest..." Miss Caroline cajoled, but there was also impatience in her tone. "Why?"

Prisca turned on her. "You wept for my father. You implored me to see you as my mother, yet you would do this thing that you know will break my heart. You take from me the only person who links me to my home. Are these the actions of a mother?"

Miss Caroline clicked her tongue. "I told your father that your attachment to the girl was unhealthy. She is a slave. A slave exists to work and be useful. She is most useful to us now in terms of the value she can bring. It is a value she should have brought three years ago, but I let my feelings for your father, and, yes, you, overshadow my good sense." Here she paused, caught her breath, and dabbed tears from her eyes. "Now you scold me for my kindness."

"Mother Caroline, there is more about this that concerns me." Every eye turned back to Master George. "Do you think Prisca does this alone, or do you think she makes plans with Lucia?"

Now I knew why George had wanted me to serve. I stepped back when his gaze fell on me.

"The two girls come from an island of slave revolt, where the natural order is reversed: slaves are the rulers through terror. So I am compelled to wonder, is it Prisca who acts so inexcusably on her own, or is it the slave girl filling Prisca's mind with such untoward actions? Until two days ago I had no reason to doubt Prisca's loyalty, but now, suddenly . . . this." He addressed Prisca directly. "Just last night I looked out to see you walking back from the slave quarters. What reason would you have to go there? Has the girl been summoning you to her defense? Has she threatened you with violence should you fail to obey her?"

Prisca opened her mouth, but for a moment no sound came out. Then she stood. "Your accusations are abhorrent to me." She slammed her hand down on the table so that her silverware jumped. "*You* are abhorrent to me."

"Abhorrent?" Miss Alice made a sound between laughter and choking. Everyone at the table froze. "Abhorrent is what my mother has been forced to endure for three years."

Prisca was startled into silence by Miss Alice's ferocity. Miss Caroline went as pale as her daughter had flushed red. "Alice, no!"

Miss Alice didn't stop. "Abhorrent is the abomination that your father brought into this home!"

She seemed to be teetering on a precipice and had taken Prisca to stand with her on the edge.

"You're mad," said Prisca, recovering herself. "What possible abomination could you associate with my father?"

Miss Alice leaned back, a serpent poised to strike.

"Do not continue to play us for fools. Do you think us all blind to the ways of the institution we live under? I saw it the minute you two set foot in my mother's house."

Prisca's face showed no further comprehension. I felt a deep and terrifying dread.

Miss Caroline grabbed her daughter's wrist. "Please, Alice, in the name of the Lord! You will make matters worse."

Miss Alice struck. "What is abhorrent is that Frederic brought his bastard child, your half sister, to live under this roof, to live in my mother's house!"

Prisca blinked, her face blank.

As for me, for the first time since being whipped, my back felt no pain, but I thought my legs would buckle. I felt hot and cold. I fled the room.

I ran through the serving room, past Rebecca, who called after me with alarm, and out into the steamy air. I couldn't breathe. The ground was sinking below me; the stars were falling above me. I collapsed. The world, my world, was upside down. I dug my hands into the dirt. I tried to hold on to something solid.

Miss Alice's words rang in my ears. *Fool. Bastard child. The institution we live under.* And then the memory of things Mama Sezelle used to intimate: *Don Federico*

thinks of you. You are important to Don Federico. Don Federico
will take care of you. . . .

And then some things deeper. The way I knew
Prisca's thoughts and feelings. When we were young,
the way it pained us to be separated. The indulgences,
small though they were, that Master Frederic sometimes accorded me and no other slave at Westin.

For the first time in my life I said the two words
out loud. "My father."

Then I spit. I could not bear to hold the phrase in
my mouth. It was the truth, but I wanted no part of
it. What kind of father raises two daughters, one free
and one a slave? What sort of man enslaves his own
daughter to be sold?

In the very same instant, Miss Alice had given me
my father and taken him away.

Rebecca was now beside me, pulling me up. "Quick,
come back inside. If they have to look for you it will
mean another whipping for sure." She pushed me
back through the door of the smoky cookhouse just
as Master George entered. He looked at us steadily
and then turned back without a word.

Rebecca looked into my eyes. "Whatever they do
to you, it will soon be a memory."

CHAPTER FOURTEEN

It was almost another two hours before I had dried and stored the last dish. As I walked back to Rebecca's cabin, the lights in the main house were being extinguished.

Prisca was lying in wait for me again, this time by the stables. She put her finger to her lips and motioned me to follow her inside. The first stall of six held her horse, Blue Boy. He nuzzled her as she opened his stall, pushed his large head away, and sat against the wall. She pulled me down next to her.

Sitting in the dark surrounded by the warm musky smell of horse manure and ripe hay, I didn't know

what to say or how to be with her. She was the same
girl I had known my whole life, yet everything about
who we were to each other had changed.

"How long have you been waiting out here for
me?" I asked.

"An hour or so," she answered in our native
tongue, not willing to risk being overheard.

I willed myself to speak. "I have known it and not
known it."

She put her hand on mine. "Me too. I have always
loved you beyond friendship."

I had nothing to give back. Did I love Prisca? I was
sure I had loved her when I thought we were both free.
Though we hadn't been equals in class, we had been
equals in choice and we chose each other. Now I was
her slave. Was loving her even a possibility anymore?

I remained silent.

She looked at me calmly, evenly. "Once they take
you, there is no guarantee I will ever be able to find
you again. I can't bear that. I am ashamed of myself. I
have been ashamed of myself for the last three years. I
did what I thought I had to do, but I did not do what
was right, even as I knew what right was."

She bowed her head. I was sure she was about
to cry, but I was wrong. The tears didn't come, and

she kept on, her voice bitter. "We have both been enslaved—me by lies and you by outright bondage."

I could only stare at her.

"I cannot blame you for your silence now. I cannot change what my father did to you, what he did to us. But I can change what will happen to you the day after tomorrow." Prisca drew a gold necklace and pendant from her dress sleeve and held it up. A ruby surrounded by small diamonds glinted in the moonlight. "I am not entirely penniless," she said, and made a hollow laughing noise. "It's not worth enough to enable me to buy you, but is more than enough to buy us passage to New York." She raised her eyes to meet mine. "I thought I was free, Lucia, but I'm not. I've been asleep, but I am awake now."

"*Now* you are awake?" I did not mean for my words to sound bitter, yet they did.

"Yes, now I am awake. Now I am prepared to fight for what I should have fought for before. I did nothing and I benefitted from what was done to you. I see that now."

"You mean, now that we are sisters? Now that we are kin? You mean it took shared blood for you to start caring about my welfare?"

Prisca looked down. "I realize how this must seem

to you, that I seek only to save my own soul from damnation, but I swear to you it is not true. I seek to do what is right because I have participated in what was wrong. If, once I secure your freedom, you no longer wish to see me, I will understand. I will not force you. But for God's sake, let me make right between us the little I can. Let me unlock the shackles my father placed upon you." She put her hands on my shoulders and delivered her final revelation. "Lucia, to do this, we must run tomorrow night." It was a question as well as a statement, and she waited for my answer.

I touched the searing welt under my heart. Running was a slim shot at freedom. Staying was a guarantee of slavery. I thought of the slave market that awaited me at Saint Augustine in a week's time. Running or staying, I would lose Horatio and Rebecca. But if I gained freedom, who knew? Perhaps fate would allow me to reach back and alter their fates as well. I nodded my assent.

She leaned closer. "Stay alert. I will call to you tomorrow after midnight, as soon as I'm sure everyone is asleep. We will take Blue Boy and ride through the night. At Mellonville I will trade in the pendant and the horse and we'll pay to join a carriage."

She continued. "Throughout, you will simply act as my slave. What could be more natural than a young woman on her way to visit an aunt in Savannah with her slave attending? No one ahead of us will ask questions, only those who follow. And we will make ourselves as plain as possible." With that, she pressed the pendant into my hand. "Sew this into your dress. If we are waylaid, it will be assumed that anything valuable is on my person."

Then she got up, brushed the straw from her skirt, and quietly slipped out of the barn. The plan was made.

I stood and put my hand against Blue Boy's flank. My heart still beat quickly, and I tried to draw calm from the horse's slow breath and loose-limbed ease. As I opened the stall door, I spotted Horatio standing in the shadows. Relief flooded me.

I took his arm and whispered, "Prisca wants us to run."

He chose his words carefully. "Miss Prisca thinks you can just go, but the paddyrollers will be after you by midmorning. If Miss Prisca run with you, she stealing Miz Caroline's property. They as likely to lock her up as kill you."

"I know that."

"You seen what they did to Sibby."

"Yes."

His words were slow and halting. "I ain't never known kin aside from my mama . . . but if I lose you, I lose my kin. But they gonna take you, one way or the other. So you run."

I took his hand in mine and held it, not wanting to let go. A sound outside caught his attention and he gently prodded me toward the barn door. "I'll sleep in the stable tomorrow night," he whispered. "I'll have the horse fresh."

Twice in three years I was being torn from a person I loved. I looked to the moon and stars and begged for a sign.

EATONVILLE

1903

CHAPTER FIFTEEN

I woke to the sun, a faint orange ball behind a dense veil of clouds. The air, thick with humidity and heat, slowed even time itself. With the fate of Eatonville hanging by a thread, I longed for my mama. I wanted to hug her and smell the reassuring scent of lye soap on her fingers. Most of all I wanted her to tell me we were gonna be safe, that we would weather this storm the same way we had weathered other storms. But Mama was out of my reach, and I out of hers, and the passage to safe harbor could not be promised.

Itching to get the day started, I nudged Zora, who was awake in a second.

"Let's get going before we catch Mama's eye," she said.

We raked the yard, threw ash in the privy, fed the chickens, and slopped the pigs without being asked. Then we wolfed down our grits and eggs and were out the door before Mrs. Hurston could finish tying Dick and John to a day of yard work.

We both kept conversation inside our own heads for most of the walk to Old Lady Bronson's house. We had seen her at Mr. Polk's a day and a half ago, but so much had happened that it felt much longer than that.

I was still putting together what Joe Clarke had said: it was in the power of the law to fix this, but white folks wouldn't let the law work for colored folks; if the law didn't work, we were at the mercy of a mob of white men who would hang a colored man for no reason at all—and do worse if they had a reason.

Old Lady Bronson's house was set in a clearing surrounded by loblolly pines—a small, tidy island set about with red clay pots growing aloe, lemongrass, dill, garlic, and sweet basil. There were others full of spiky- and smooth-leaved herbs and plants I didn't know the names of. Her porch was strung with flame vine. Despite its beauty, most folks thought of flame vine as a pest because it spreads fast as wildfire, but the vine on Old Lady Bronson's porch was the picture of good behavior, hanging like perfectly combed hair, its blossoms falling like crimson streaks from the sun itself. We walked up the steps to the screen door and met Old Lady Bronson about to leave on the other side, a black satchel over her shoulder, her hair in a long silver braid.

She opened the door and stepped out, her eyes sharp as an osprey's. "I expect this isn't a social call, am I right?"

Zora and I glanced at each other and back at her. Without softening her gaze, she motioned for us to sit down on the steps. "Out with it. I don't have time to waste on girlish foolishness."

"You gotta save Eatonville," Zora blurted out.

Old Lady Bronson cocked her head. "Eatonville? Now, how in the world did a whole town come to lay its troubles at your door, small fry?"

Zora told all about last night's meeting, and Old Lady Bronson's face grew dark with the telling. When Zora was done, the old woman's mouth was tight.

"Polk thought he'd scared Peterson off. I should have known that was dream-thinking." She spat on the ground. "He must not know I'm here," she muttered, but not to us. "After all these years, he must think I'm dead."

Zora straightened her back and raised her voice, reminding Old Lady Bronson that we were still there. "If you had let us tell what happened to Mr. Polk, maybe folks could have talked to him sooner."

"What do you mean, child?"

"I know Mr. Polk is protecting the land, but it's not worth my daddy's life or anybody else's. It's not too late. You can get him to sell it. *You* can talk to him—he'll listen to you. If he sells it to that white man, Mr. Clarke and my daddy and brothers and all the other men won't have to risk their lives protecting him tonight." If desperation could carry the day, there would have been no refusing her.

"That white man doesn't want to buy the land. He wants to take it. And Polk will never let that land go, not as long as he's breathing air." Old Lady Bronson spoke in a voice as flat as if she'd just told us the sky was gray.

"But why? There ain't nothing out there but an old plantation house almost swallowed up by the woods! Why would he want to save a place where white folks kept slaves?"

Old Lady Bronson looked at Zora sharply. "How do you come to know what's on Polk's land?"

Zora was bolder by the minute. "We found it yesterday, looking for Moss Star. Please, Miz Bronson, please talk to him. Why does he want to keep that land when he doesn't even use it?"

Old Lady Bronson passed her hand over her eyes. "Believe it or not, that place was home to Polk and me for many sad years."

Zora and I startled like squirrels.

"You and Mr. Polk lived in that house?" I blurted. It made no sense to me.

She nodded grimly. "We were slaves. The Westin place was a plantation when we were young. It was our prison and our hell here on earth."

I couldn't believe it. I felt my throat closing up.

"Then why not get rid of it?" Zora demanded. "Why keep any part of slavery close to you, especially if it can hurt Eatonville?"

Old Lady Bronson looked sadder than I've ever seen a grown person look. "Horatio and I made a mistake. We thought knowledge of what happened on that land was ours alone. We thought that by not speaking about it we could keep the poison waters of slavery from spoiling the new well of Eatonville. We were wrong. We thought we were protecting Eatonville from knowledge of a horrible past, but we were really protecting ourselves from the pain of our own memories." And here she hung her head in shame. "The past is living in each one of us. Trying to push it down below remembering just makes it find another way through."

She looked at Zora. "I owe you an apology. You were right to want to tell. I was wrong to bind you to my secret. I don't know that telling could have done any good, but not telling has surely made things worse."

Old Lady Bronson sat down between us and pulled us against her with strong hands. I could feel the rapid beat of her heart beneath the rough linen of her indigo dress, and I finally understood something. I had always thought Old Lady Bronson was a witch, and so I feared her strength and power. But all that time, she was just a woman, filled with the same vulnerability, pain, and misery life holds for each of us. I reached out my arm and wrapped it around her waist.

"Listen," she said. "There is one person in Lake Maitland who may have some influence over the white folks there, but I need the two of you to work with me. You know where Mr. Ambrose lives?" We nodded. "I'm going to write a letter, and I want you to take it to him as fast as you can. Hear me?"

"Yes'm," we said.

She gave us a tight squeeze to emphasize her point, then was up and back inside her house with the energy of a woman half her age.

She reappeared a few minutes later with a sealed envelope and pushed the letter into Zora's hand. "Now, run!" And with that she shoved us one way while she hurried off in the other direction.

We were slow to get going at first. I think we were both too dazed to make our feet move. Zora looked down at the envelope. It was addressed to Jude Ambrose.

"Jude," Zora said. "I've been knowing Mr. Ambrose all my life, but I never thought about him having a first name."

My thoughts drifted back to Mr. Polk's property and the plantation house we had stood in. "I keep thinking about Old Lady Bronson and Mr. Polk on that plantation," I said. "As slaves."

"Me too. It pains me to think of it."

"Mama and I live in the same house we lived in with my daddy, and everything reminds me of him every day. You think it's like that for her and Mr. Polk? You think all of Eatonville reminds them of when they were slaves?"

"It seems like it must," Zora answered. "It must hurt something awful."

"If I had lived on that plantation, I would have torn it down by now," I all but spat. "I would have burned that rotten house down to the ground."

Zora tilted her head like she was listening to a thought from far away. "Maybe. But maybe burning it would feel like burning their memories."

"But why would you want to remember such a painful memory? Something that took your freedom away?"

"Maybe they don't think of it like that," she said. "Maybe they see that house and think about a part of their life that's gone. If they destroyed it, every bit of that life would disappear, like a piece of themselves. Maybe they need something from that house. Maybe Mr. Polk is trying to hold on to something more than land."

I couldn't imagine what they would need from such a torturous past, but Zora's argument held a kernel of truth I could not deny. I always hated visiting my father's cousin Elsie — she was so crotchety and mean—but without her I would never have learned about the peach tree my father planted as a child, or tasted its sweet fruit. And now that my father was gone, Cousin Elsie's peach tree was one of the few tangible things I had left of him. Whenever we visited her and I ate those peaches, I could see my father's smiling face—for one delicious moment I had him back. No amount of pain caused by Elsie's ceaseless complaining and chastising could make me give up my father's peaches. Maybe it was like that for Old Lady Bronson and Mr. Polk. They had to keep the horrible to hold on to something good.

"Yet and still," I said, "I hate thinking of them chained up as some white person's property. I can't begin to imagine Old Lady Bronson without her fishing pole, popping up anywhere you least expect her. And how could someone have owned Mr. Polk the same way he owns his horses? I hate the whole idea of it."

"Maybe that's the problem. Old Lady Bronson thought Mr. Polk's story and her story were theirs to keep, but they're not. Don't you see? Their stories are Eatonville's stories, Eatonville's history. I thought history was something in books, but it's not. History is alive. Old Lady Bronson and Mr. Polk are living history."

I had thought Zora was looking to solve a puzzle for the past two days. What she had really been doing was piecing together a quilt, made from the fleeting scraps of the said and the unsaid. She was starting to unfold and show us a whole cloth of Eatonville's history.

As we hurried along the road to Lake Maitland, Zora's words sank in deeper and deeper. Old Lady Bronson and Mr. Polk had been slaves right here in Eatonville, the first incorporated colored town in America. Eatonville, a place I couldn't even associate with white folks, let alone slavery, was the same place that had enslaved folks we knew. Zora was right: history wasn't just something you read in a book. It was everything your life stood on. We who thought we were free from the past were still living it out.

We walked without another word until we got to the heart of Lake Maitland, where Mr. Ambrose's house stood.

WESTIN

1855

CHAPTER SIXTEEN

As night approached on the day of our escape, I could barely contain my nerves. Rebecca brought me a plate of hominy and eyed me sharply when I dropped it. "I don't care much for food tonight," I mumbled. Guilt at deceiving her tightened my stomach. After Horatio, she was the person I cared for most. She had never failed to help me find my footing in this cruel new world. She had ministered to my physical wounds like a tender mother. If I told her what I was going to do, she'd be carrying a deadly secret. To protect her I would confide nothing. When

Master George questioned her, she must be able to answer honestly.

Shortly after supper, she lay down on her pallet and began her prayers. I extinguished our one candle and did the same. My heart beat like a wild drum. Soon she was breathing rhythmically, and I lay kitty-corner to her, my eyes open wide, listening to sounds that weren't there. Now I only had to feign sleep for two hours. I prayed Rebecca would sleep soundly.

Time never moved more slowly. With each passing moment, my hope slid toward terror as I imagined the horrors that awaited us if we were caught: Prisca imprisoned; me whipped to death. My mouth was dead-leaf dry, but I dared not stir or drink from the gourd. Any noise risked waking Rebecca.

At last I heard the sound I had been waiting for: the call of the white-necked crow. It was the sound of our island; no bird here uttered such a lilting call. I sat up and listened carefully to be sure that nothing else stirred. Then I stood. When I looked over at Rebecca to be sure she still slept, I startled. Her eyes were wide open! She put her finger to her lips and rose from her pallet as silently as a cat. From her skirt she took a little bundle. It was bread. She must have baked an extra loaf during the day. She pushed it into my hands, hugged me roughly, and lay back down. She turned onto her side, face toward the wall and her back to me.

I felt so much love for her in that moment that I wanted to weep. They could beat us, they could sell our loved ones away from us, but they could not reach our souls. They could not destroy our hope for others even when we could not hope for ourselves.

I opened the door and slipped outside. Prisca, in a full riding habit, emerged from behind a pine tree and we made our way to the stables. True to his word, Horatio was waiting there with Blue Boy. The glistening black horse had been fed, watered, and saddled.

Prisca thanked Horatio with tears in her eyes, for he was facilitating her escape every bit as much as my own. I think it was the first time that she was fully seeing him. Until then, I don't think she had ever truly seen any slave at Westin. Such is the power of human bondage to blind the mind.

As she packed a small bundle into the saddlebag, I went over to Horatio. I took his hands in mine. As with Rebecca, I had no words.

"Got to be quick," Horatio said to us. To Prisca, he said, "Walk the horse on the grass out to the gate. Mount him there." Prisca nodded.

No sooner had Horatio given the reins to Prisca than a shaky voice echoed in the barn.

"You let go my papa's property!"

From behind another stall stepped Timothy, pointing a rifle at us, his face looking particularly small behind the dark stock.

We froze. I couldn't breathe. He had spied on Prisca the time she'd spoken to Jude about marriage, he had followed her again tonight. This time, I could tell he would not be satisfied with merely reporting what he'd heard or learned. Timothy was no older than me and Horatio, yet he stood like an insurmountable wall between us and freedom.

His voice sharpened even as it quavered. "Horatio, you let that horse go. Lucia, you come round here where I am."

Not one of us moved. It was as if we were in a trance.

He spoke louder. "You hear me? You do as I say. Now!"

Prisca laughed. "Timothy, honestly, you scared us half to death!" Her tone was light, but her eyes were dark. "Now, hand me that thing before someone gets hurt."

I could see that her teasing tone only made him

angrier. I wanted to go to her, take her arm, tell her it was already over, but I couldn't—they were still talking, and time was moving faster than my thoughts could make themselves real.

Timothy kicked at some straw. "My papa will make Krowse whip you, too, Prisca," he warned. "You see if he doesn't."

"I have no patience for your childishness." Despite her long dress, Prisca was upon him in a few steps. With her left hand she snatched the rifle, and with her right she slapped Timothy's face so hard the sound echoed off the barn walls.

Timothy touched his cheek. His face burned the bright color of a winter apple.

"Childishness," she said again, tossing the rifle atop a stack of hay bales against the wall. "Now, you stand there, and not a word until I tell you to speak, understand?"

Anything Prisca may have understood about slavery had flown from her mind the moment Timothy challenged her authority and her seniority. He was a boy—two years younger than she was—so Prisca failed to recognize the power he had just for being the son of Master George.

Every slave on the plantation, however, recognized

it. Horatio's mind was faster than mine; he leaped for the gun before any words of caution could even leave my mouth. Timothy and Horatio reached the weapon at almost the same instant, but Timothy was a hairbreadth closer. He grabbed the rifle and spun around, hitting Horatio above the right eye with the butt. Horatio lurched sideways with the impact and then fell to his knees, his hands on his bloody head.

I turned to stone.

Prisca turned on Timothy. "You little beast!" she snarled, and moved toward him again, her hands outstretched for the gun.

Timothy made a strangled sound. Then he began to sob. His hands were shaking, too, but he turned the rifle around expertly, raised it, and took aim. Only then did Prisca register the hate that lived in him, the hate that every slave at Westin knew. But it was too late. I had known it was too late from the moment she slapped him.

"Put the gun down, Timothy," she said more gently. "This is a mistake. You don't understand what you're seeing here. No one is taking anything."

Timothy yelled one word. "No!"

Prisca moved again, her arm out. She was only

inches away from the end of the gun when a hot *pop* burst the air.

Horatio dropped his bloody hands and looked up at me, trying to figure out what had just happened. He and I locked eyes for a moment, and then we heard the sound—something solid slipping heavily to the hay-strewn floor.

I dropped to the floor and crawled the few feet to Prisca, cradling her head in my lap. Blood was pooling across her chest and down the fabric of her dress.

Hermana, hermana, I cried in Spanish. *Hermana, hermana, hermana.* I screamed so long it became a wail.

I became aware of voices from outside, yelling, drawing nearer. The stable door exploded open and there stood Master George, nightshirt over his pants, eyes wild, a long pistol raised. Mr. Krowse ran up behind him, similarly disheveled, holding a carbine.

Master George looked from Timothy to Horatio, who had made his way over to me, and from Horatio to me, holding Prisca in my arms. I saw the dawning realization focus Master George's gaze. He swung to face Timothy again. "What happened here, boy?"

Before Timothy could answer, Blue Boy began to gasp and paw at the floor. I had the fleeting impression that he was grieving his mistress, but then his knees buckled, and I saw the blood and understood. He was suffering. The bullet had gone straight through Prisca and landed in Blue Boy's neck. His eyes rolled back wildly. He could no longer draw breath. He shook his great head, refusing, like all living things, to accept that his time had come. Then his head dropped to the ground. His eye looked at us, and stopped moving.

George was sweating. I could see it glistening on his forehead in the soft light cast by Horatio's lantern. The scene was so gentle, the light so golden, the other horses snorting so softly, it could almost have been a manger scene. But instead of new life and a hopeful start, this was a tableau of fresh death and the end of hope.

"Prisca was fixing to run off with Lucia," Timothy was saying between sobs. "I saw them, Papa. Horatio, he was helping them. I . . . I stopped them."

Master George took hold of his son's arm. "Give me the gun, son."

When George had the gun in his hands, he held the barrel up to his nose and smelled it. Then he walked over to us. "Is she dead?" His voice was matter-of-fact, though the hand that held the gun shook slightly.

I couldn't register the question, much less voice an answer. I knew when I touched her that there was no hope. She was gone by the time I had cradled her head. My own dress was soaked in blood and she still bled.

I pointed at Timothy, and what came out of me was a shriek. "He killed my sister!"

I screamed again, and then again, the sounds coming up from deep inside.

George leaned down and slapped me to make me stop screaming. I tasted my own salty blood.

Now the only sound in the barn was Timothy's sobs.

George's hands were no longer shaking, but his voice was ragged. "Timothy did not kill her, you hear?"

I looked up into his face and his whole intention became clear. He was not thinking of Prisca or about the fact that she had just been killed. He was thinking only of how he would protect Timothy and himself, of how he would hide the fact that his son was a murderer.

And then I was floating and the room was falling away. From up in the roof beams, I looked down and watched myself settle Prisca's body gently on the hay.

I watched myself stand, my hands red, my dress heavy with blood.

That's when Mama Sezelle and the old women of my island began whispering old words in my ears. And as their words came to me, I floated back down to the ground. I pointed my finger at the father and then I pointed my finger at the son, and I spoke the words. I spoke in a voice I had never heard, in a whisper so cold and distant it seemed to come from underground. "I call on the gods of my land, and the gods of my ancestors. I call on every power of this world. I call on the spirits who move among us, and I curse you and yours. I curse your name that it be a sign of shame. And I curse the land under your feet that it fall fallow and yield nothing as long as you live."

I flicked blood on the ground at the feet of the boy and spat in it. I flicked blood on the ground at the feet of the father and spat in it. With my heel I ground it into the dirt.

Alice and Caroline were at the stable door by then, watching. Alice had her hand over her mouth. And I caught a glimpse of Rebecca hiding in the shadows behind them. For a long moment, no one moved or spoke. Then George slapped me so hard I fell.

He turned to Horatio. "What did you see, boy?"

It was equal parts threat and demand. "What did you see?"

Horatio was staring at the scene, but no words left his lips. No words then. No words since.

George pushed Timothy toward Krowse, who had been watching the scene with his gun at the ready. Krowse moved quickly to herd the boy and the two women out of the barn. Timothy held on to Alice's hand, wailing like a small child. Rebecca must have hidden herself. I prayed they had not seen her. George closed the stable doors behind them. I could see that his hands trembled again. He stepped quickly over to Horatio and knocked him down with a blow twice as hard as the one he had dealt me.

His voice was thick, and it faltered. "You don't want to tell me what you saw? That's fine. I'm going to tell *you* what you saw, and you're going to tell it back to me, just the way you heard it." Now his voice rose with urgency. "'I was mucking out the stalls,' you'll say, 'but bad luck, because just then, just then, horse thieves bust in.' Horse thieves! And they beat you on the head. 'Then Miss Prisca came in to see her horse; she came in with her slave girl Lucia—'" He stopped, scanned the room before he continued.

187

"No. No slave girl. 'Prisca came in alone. She tried to keep the thieves from taking her horse, but one of them shot her. In cold blood! They shot the horse, too, and then they ran off. That's when I came running in, but it was too late—the horse thieves were gone and Miss Prisca was dead!'" He pulled Horatio up by the shirt so they were face-to-face. "Now say it back to me."

Horatio didn't answer. He didn't even acknowledge that George had spoken. He just stared at Prisca, at her empty body.

George raised his voice. "I said, say it back to me!" Horatio ignored him still. George kicked Horatio so hard then that he closed his eyes. He grunted, too, but still he didn't speak.

"You see that, George?" I hissed.

He spun around to me.

"Your power over us will end."

"Nothing will end, you witch!" He moved toward me.

But I no longer cared about the power he held over my body. Hope makes you believe the body can be protected, but I had no more hope.

I looked him right in the eye. "You're not my master. I have no master, George."

Rage flushed his face and he grabbed me by the arm. I fell and he dragged me out of the stable and across the long yard to the smokehouse. He undid the latch, threw me inside, and slammed the door shut.

That week I learned the contours of hell. The smokehouse was a small structure, maybe nine feet by nine feet, made of thick Florida oak. In late fall when pigs of the right age were slaughtered, the sides of meat were salted and hung to dry for a couple of weeks as a low fire burned in the corner, then they were moved to the side enclosure to be kept until needed. On the first morning I was locked in there, a small fire had been set to continue smoking a few birds that were hung, and mercifully, the fire was only hours away from reaching the last glow of its embers. But in those first few hours, the thick smoke burned so hot it closed my eyes and dried up any tears I might have had left. I lay flat on the floor, trying to get as far below the smoke as I could, but it filled every inch of the small round dwelling. It seared my lungs, each breath like molten glass. The smoky nettles moved into my clothes and penetrated the raw lashes on my back, but I did not cry, I did not wail, and I did not pity myself. Prisca was dead—what was there to pity?

I cried for Prisca and prayed for Horatio's safety. I thought about the story George commanded Horatio to tell. If Horatio kept his silence, maybe George would curtail his punishment, but even as I allowed for the thought, I knew it was a fantasy. George would level his rage on Horatio as brutally as he did on me. A slave's complicity in escape was as grave a crime as the actual escape.

By the second day the fire pit had burned out and I continued in darkness. I could tell night from day only by the smallest slivers of light where the blackened boards were not completely flush. Even with the fire out, the tin roof heated the tight space like an oven, and night cooled it only by scant degrees.

Three salted and smoked wild turkeys hanging in the smokehouse fed my hunger but also exacerbated my thirst. My thirst became so deep that I barely passed water. I began sucking on my own hand.

Hate blossomed in my chest. I fantasized death and destruction. My grieving was displaced by rage, and through raging I felt no more pain, only the pandemonium of loathing, the blind ferocity of a rabid creature. Horatio's words came back to me: *Hate too hard and it'll steal the memory of what you love. Hate long enough, and you won't feel nothing for no one.*

On the third day, parched, I became feverish. In my delirium, I visited Mama Sezelle on our island; I watched my own whipping; I ran along the beach with Prisca; I floated over Prisca's body; I played with my wooden doll while listening intently to and absorbing Prisca's daily lessons; I watched Horatio run his work-roughened fingers over words in a reader I had stolen for him. Once I even lay in a cradle and looked up at Don Federico's enormous, sad face, looming over me like the moon. I don't know how long I had been drifting when Prisca began to sing, her voice coming from somewhere just above me. I opened my eyes. I called her name. Only darkness and silence.

I closed my eyes again and her song returned. I struggled to my knees, then stood, legs shaking, hands reaching out to find her. I clutched only air, and I slumped back down to the ground. Her song continued. It was a melody from our childhood, a song Mama Sezelle taught us when we were either side of five.

Now I saw that Horatio was right. Consumed by hate, I was losing myself. But memory was my defense. Rooted in love, it was stronger than hate.

I felt things I had not felt for a long time. I remembered Mama Sezelle. I remembered her last words to me. I remembered that on the island the old women drew the wisdom from the natural world. How the *cacata* plays dead to escape a predator. How parched milkweed seeds hold themselves in the ground, small and tight, until the rains come. I closed my eyes and I curled myself into a tight ball against the earthen floor. I would be a milkweed seed; I would hold myself tight and refuse to die. Hate was my shield, but it would not be my essence. Prisca had staked her life to free me. I would not die.

On the fourth day, the day after Prisca was buried, George Peterson opened the door, dragged me out, and threw me at Rebecca's feet. He uttered only one sentence. "Tell her what talking will bring."

Rebecca looked upon me with glassy eyes and, once again, tended to my broken body.

The next day I saw Horatio. He had received the lash twenty times, and still he would not speak. Ignoring his own pain and the risk he was taking, he snuck into Rebecca's cabin to see me. He propped me up and helped me drink water from a gourd but said not a word.

Rebecca was almost as mute as Horatio, but mouthed "Hush" nervously when I uttered Prisca's name. When I begged her to speak to me, her response was a frightened whisper. "Samuel is all the kin I got left. If Master George sells him, I got nothing left on this earth. If you care about us that's still alive, you will put that night away. Put it away like we've all had to put away the folks we loved. Lock it in a room inside yourself and hide the key." She pointed at my heart, at Horatio's heart, and then at her own. "What you and I know won't bring no justice outside these walls."

A month later George sent Timothy and Alice to tie up loose ends in Saint Augustine. It was Mitilde— a girl of nineteen who picked with a stubborn slowness no matter how many times Krowse used the lash—who they took to sell instead of me. Seems my tongue was deemed too great a risk to set loose.

Prisca's death caused unease among the whites throughout the county and beyond. Uneasy whites always bring black death. Patrols were doubled and more poor whites were made patrollers. Fear in the slave cabins was so thick you could taste it.

The horse thieves George claimed had taken Prisca's life were never seen again, but that didn't lessen the vigilance and suspicion that gripped the area. Rather, stories of murderous bandits and rebellious slaves only seemed to flourish and grow in the minds of white folks, and they clutched their guns ever more tightly.

I wasn't sold, but I was put to work in the fields. Krowse, who had been rewarded for his loyalty with a new horse, would find reason every day to deliver a lash to my back. My fingers, unaccustomed to the work, were slow and clumsy, and they bled from the effort of pulling thorny fluffs of cotton from their sticky casings.

The other slaves gave me wide berth, lest any gesture toward me invite the lash. Their glances were fearful as they passed me, their bags bulging with cotton while mine was barely half full after a whole day's labor. I'm sure they had their own suspicions about what might have happened to Prisca, but after her death and burial, no slave dared risk invoking her.

Two years later, when Prisca's death had shrunk to be of no greater consequence than a drunkard knifing his neighbor over a card game, George sold me as a field hand to a plantation six miles down the road. I'm sure I commanded but a modest price, small as I was and my face a studied mask of nothing.

Three months into my life on the new plantation,

I tended to a particularly bad whipping. After that, my fellow slaves came to me with their wounds and their aches. Word spread that I had a gift. Folks even whispered that I had the power to sit by the door of death and keep it locked out on the other side. I listened to the old slaves, absorbed the wisdom that had traveled with them from the old countries. I learned the names and uses of every herb and plant that grew. Often I tried remedies on myself first—many a night I spent vomiting when a mixture I made had not yet found the right balance.

I began to see medicine in part as an art, and in part as a sleight of hand. I gave people herbs to bring better function to the body, and I mixed them with visions of the future to kindle hope—a yeast to the medicine itself. It was the visions that folks remembered, whether or not I could heal their bodies, and so a reputation began to spread around me, one that increased the hope I represented by seasoning it with fear. I became known as a conjure woman, a seer, a hoodoo woman.

Over the years I followed the news at Westin through Mary, a cousin of Rebecca's who was often loaned out to sew delicate lace at the surrounding plantations. She told me that Rebecca brought the child of Samuel and his wife into the world. She told me that Rebecca watched Samuel and the child later get sold west to a place in Louisiana or Mississippi. Once a year, Mary would bring me a piece of paper folded and tied with string: a letter to me from Horatio. Rather than write about himself, he wrote out poems we'd memorized together when we were young. It was a kind of code; it was his way of letting me know that they had yet to break what was at the center of him.

Through Mary I learned that Caroline was taken by yellow fever and that Alice died from an infected knee, the amputation coming too late to save her. Four years after that, she brought the news that George had been kicked in the chest and killed by the same horse that had caused Timothy to break his toe. For the five years since Prisca's death, frost or some other blight wrecked the cotton and newly planted sugarcane at Westin, though curiously it afflicted no place else, at least not to the same degree. I felt no joy hearing any of this, only a quiet satisfaction in knowing that my words had been an instrument for justice.

Toward the end of 1860, just as rumors of war against the government were becoming more rampant, word came to me that Horatio had escaped. I was filled with joy. I lay awake at night praying to every god whose name I knew for him to make it north.

The war did come in 1861, and Timothy, nineteen years old then, purchased a captaincy in the Confederacy. Before he left Westin, he hired out every slave he owned to the surrounding farms and plantations and used the human rent to maintain him. Rebecca was rented out to my plantation. The day she was delivered by cart I ran to her. She was a ghost of her former self, thin, sickly, and weak. I spent weeks coaxing her away from death's door.

In 1865 the war ended and we slaves were declared free. Rebecca and I walked off that plantation with nothing but the clothes on our backs. We traveled back to Westin, and there squatted on the abandoned land, free women. Rebecca lived two years as a free woman before sickness took her.

Horatio had joined the Union army and fought in the war. After the war, he worked as a blacksmith for a wage in Saint Augustine for three years. Then, like me, the ghosts of his past whispered to him to turn back, and we were reunited in 1868.

Almost twenty years later, a brash young man named Joe Clarke established the charter for an all-colored town called Eatonville. He knocked on my door one morning to ask if I wouldn't mind letting him build a colored town on the land around my home. He was a man with charm and a vision that could not be denied. I thrilled to his vision and looked forward to seeing the blighted land of Westin engulfed by a town that freedom built.

Horatio was the first to buy into Eatonville. With the money he had saved working in Saint Augustine, he bought outright the land that had once been the Westin plantation and the small plot of land my home stood on. Joe Clarke, a straight shooter, urged him to reconsider; the land was known to be fallow. But Horatio had made up his mind. That same day Horatio put the deeds in my hands, he spoke the only words I had heard him utter since the night Prisca died. "So no one can take from us again."

One who did not return after the war was Timothy Peterson. No one in these parts had heard from him since he left for the war — not after the war, not when Westin was declared abandoned, not when it was being turned into Eatonville, not anytime after. I believed that, like so many white men of the South, he had given his life for the cause of owning other human beings. I whispered my belief to Prisca's grave one lonely night, but no sound came back, no sign. I looked around at the fallow land then, and a seed of comprehension slowly germinated: the land was still bearing my curse. If my curse was still working, that meant that Timothy Peterson was still alive.

EATONVILLE

1903

CHAPTER SEVENTEEN

ora stood on her toes and knocked with the big brass lion's head that adorned Mr. Ambrose's front door. It would never occur to us to go to the front door of any other white folks in the world, but with Mr. Ambrose, it would never occur to us not to.

I remember Mr. Hurston once saying that being friends with a white man is a dangerous proposition, but we couldn't imagine anything dangerous about Mr. Ambrose. Unlike the other white men we saw on occasion, Mr. Ambrose moved as easily in Eatonville as he did in Lake Maitland. Whether coming to fish or just passing through, folks respected and accepted him. He, in turn, tended to bring out the best in folks. I had always liked him, but he won my unbreakable trust two years earlier when he helped prevent a murderer from slipping through the hands of the law. Mr. Ambrose had helped Mr. Clarke restore a quiet justice to Eatonville, and I looked on him as a friend ever since.

After a minute the door was opened by Millie, who had a baby tied to her back. Mr. Ambrose had never married, so he always hired someone to cook and clean for him. For the last few years it had been Millie, who came early every morning and went back to her husband and children on the other side of Lake Maitland in the evening. We knew her by sight, like we knew every colored person within a five-mile radius.

"Hi, Millie," we chimed.

She frowned to see us, even as her daughter gurgled and banged her little nut-brown fists happily against Millie's back. "Something happen in Eatonville?" Her aunt lived on the other side of Joe Clarke and her mind must have gone to her the minute she laid eyes on us. Why would we be there but as harbingers of crisis? Unfortunately, she was right.

"We got a letter for Mr. Ambrose," Zora explained.

Millie opened the door for us to enter, her expression unchanged. Mr. Ambrose appeared from behind her, full of hearty cheer as usual.

"Snidlets! And Carrie! This is a pleasant surprise. I don't think you've ever visited me at home before. Have I gone too long without fishing at the Blue Sink?" His eyes were warm and welcoming, as they always were whenever he saw Zora.

Mr. Ambrose had happened by and helped Lucy Hurston when she found herself alone with Zora deciding to get born early. He had even cut the umbilical cord. After that he'd made it his business to inquire after Zora's health regularly and keep up with her as she grew. He'd called her Snidlets since any of us could remember.

Zora handed him the letter.

"A letter! Why, this gets more mysterious by the minute!"

"It's from Old Lady Bronson," Zora quickly added.

No sooner had the name left her mouth than his smile faded and his brow creased. He tore open the letter and read silently and quickly. Then he sat down heavily in one of the chairs that lined the long hallway.

"This is bad news you bring me, Snidlets. Bad news indeed."

"We know, Mr. Ambrose. My daddy says men are going to ride on Eatonville. Is that true? Would white folks from Lake Maitland ride on us?"

Sorrowfully, Mr. Ambrose nodded.

"But why?" Zora insisted. "Why would white folks who been living peacefully one town over want to hurt us now?"

I jumped in. "Mr. Clarke says Mr. Polk owns the land by law, but that the law won't work for us on account of race."

Mr. Ambrose nodded again. "There's no law in this country that will help a colored man keep something a white man says belongs to *him*."

"My daddy said the same thing," Zora said. "But slavery is over. Why white folks don't got to respect the law when it comes to us?"

"The law is reasonable when reasonable men practice it," he answered. "But when it comes to color, there are very few reasonable men."

"You're reasonable," Zora pushed. "How come other white men aren't?"

Mr. Ambrose rubbed his forehead, then said, "Because slavery isn't far enough in our past yet. What we're facing now is the unfinished business of that slavery."

"When *will* it be finished?" Zora demanded.

"That's what I want to know," I added.

"I don't know, girls. White folks have a disease. A disease that started with slavery. We taught ourselves to see colored folks as inferior so we could enslave them. And now we have a *need* to keep seeing them as inferior. White folks have become dependent on feeling superior to the colored race; no matter how low we fall, we can tell ourselves that the colored man is always lower."

"Do you think that, too?" Zora asked.

Mr. Ambrose took a full minute to respond. "It would be a lie to say I didn't. Every white man I know has the seed of race hate planted and rooted in him by the time he's reached his fifth year. This country is founded on it, and not even a civil war could uproot it. The only way to fight that hate is to consciously decide every day to choose against the hate we've been taught."

He looked from Zora to me, his eyes speaking sadness. "I wish it hadn't taken me so long to understand that," he went on. "I joined up to fight in the war like the young fool I was, more fired up with notions of valor and glory than anything else. I saw glory disappear in the first few months. More I slowly came to wonder at the point of valor in a cause I could not justify. Spring of sixty-three found me in Louisiana, at Port Hudson. Ever heard about Port Hudson?"

We shook our heads. We knew our states and their capitals, but less about the rest. He smiled grimly.

"The Union had us under siege. We were starving, reduced to eating our mules. The only thing we hadn't run out of was gunpowder. We had no way to treat our wounded, so *wounded* just meant slow death. We had been told the fort we were in was unassailable, but the Union blew it to pieces bit by bit. One night in late June, after endless artillery pounding, there was an infantry assault. Men I knew fell all around me, yet no bullet claimed me. A mortar shell sent me flying. When I came to, I tried to get up and run, but I tripped over the body of the man lying next to me. As I got to my knees, I felt a gun barrel pressed to my forehead. I froze. The soldier pointing a musket at me was a colored boy, not yet old enough to grow a beard, in a Union uniform two sizes too big. He looked at me, and I saw myself in his eyes: a Confederate officer fighting to stay alive so I could go on keeping him a slave. If I had been in his shoes, I would have pulled the trigger, but he hesitated. I could tell he didn't have killing in him. A shot rang out from somewhere behind me and I threw myself flat on the ground. When I raised my head, I was alive and the boy was dead. Shot dead because he didn't shoot me first."

Mr. Ambrose held his head in his hands.

"Two weeks later our commanding officer surrendered. The surviving officers were sent to Johnson's Island, where we spent the rest of the war. But in the early rays of morning after that boy's death, I made a promise to God. I told Him that if He saw fit to spare my life, I would honor Him by never using my life as anything other than an instrument of peace. And to this day, I have never gone back on my promise to Him."

Zora reached out and put her hand on Mr. Ambrose's arm.

Mr. Ambrose patted her hand with affection, even as his face remained drenched in sadness. "Listen, I need to talk to some folks, even though I doubt it will do any good. You two hurry home and keep your wits about you. You see white folks coming, you hide right quick, hear me? You hide!"

The urgency in his voice told us that what Joe Clarke and Mr. Hurston feared was surely coming to pass.

He put on his jacket, ushered us down the steps, and, just like Old Lady Bronson had done, nudged us in one direction while he hurried off in another.

CHAPTER EIGHTEEN

Zora and I walked home from Mr. Ambrose's place, our thoughts heavy.

"Hey, you two!" I looked up to see Micah and Teddy coming our way. My heart gave an involuntary skip at the sight of Teddy, and I had to remind myself that I was still angry with him for saying I had tried to kiss him when it was him just as much as me.

Zora sped up to meet them. "Where y'all going?"

Teddy looked down and Micah answered. "Moss Star is down the road a bit. I think his leg might be broken. He's too skittish for me to get close, so Teddy's coming to see to him."

I looked at Teddy and my heart melted. Knowing how much Teddy hated to see any animal suffer, I knew it had to be even more unbearable when it was one that held his heart, like Moss Star.

About a year earlier, Teddy's oldest brother, Jake, had clipped a hedgehog with his hoe, tearing a gash in its soft belly. Teddy had leaped to save the creature. Jake and Mr. Baker told him the animal would die, but Teddy refused the fact with the will of a sentry standing guard. He stayed by the hedgehog night and day, cleaning its wound, feeding it, and on the fourth day it rose like Lazarus from the dead. Teddy took the healed creature outside and set it down at the edge of the field.

As Jake liked to tell the tale afterward, the hedgehog ran into the field without even a backward glance: "'So much for all your effort, Teddy!' Daddy told him. But Teddy, he just said, 'You don't save a life for it to be beholden to you. You save a life because your heart tells you to.' I can tell you," Jake said, "that was the last time any of us ever told Teddy he couldn't heal anything."

I stood with the Bakers on that. I truly believed that there was no animal, sick or hurt, that Teddy couldn't fix.

"Come on, Teddy. We'll go with you," I said, taking Zora's hand.

Zora grabbed Teddy's arm and we walked on until we got to a stand of holly trees. There stood Moss Star. Normally regal, his posture was slightly off-balance. His mane, always so smooth and fine, looked like straw. He was holding up his right front leg, almost like a pointer dog. When he caught sight of Teddy, he nickered and bobbed his head up and down.

Teddy slowed way down and stepped steadily toward Moss Star while Zora and I waited a ways off so as not to spook him. Moss Star stayed right where he was until Teddy reached him. Then Teddy began to caress his neck and speak to him softly. Moss Star nuzzled Teddy's cheek in return. Then Teddy bent down and stroked the top of Moss Star's leg, making sure the horse settled enough before touching the injury. After gently probing the lower part of the leg, Teddy stood back up and put his arms around Moss Star's neck. The two of them stood like that for several minutes, Moss Star curving his neck around Teddy so they were embracing like old friends. When Teddy walked back to us, he had tears in his eyes.

"You were right, Micah," he said. "The leg's broke."

"No!" I whispered. "No, no, no." Now that Moss Star had shifted position, I could just make out a small white bone jutting through his skin. Surely such a small thing could be fixed. It couldn't possibly bring something as momentous as death with it. Why, there wasn't even any blood.

Teddy reached for the shotgun in Micah's hands, but Micah said, "Let me do this. You take the girls and go home."

Teddy shook his head. "Moss Star is my friend. I promised Mr. Polk I would find him and bring him home."

Micah put his hand on Teddy's neck in a brotherly way. "OK," he said. "You do it right." They walked to the horse together. Micah pulled a length of fabric from his overalls pocket and handed it to Teddy.

Teddy wrapped the cloth around Moss Star's head like a big blindfold, all the while murmuring, soothing. Meanwhile, Micah loaded the shotgun with two shells the size of his thumbs and passed the gun to Teddy. I watched Teddy's slender brown hands cradle the shotgun and nestle it into his shoulder. This boy, who wanted no part of guns, knew how to handle one as well as his brother. Teddy was raised to use guns, yet I had never seen him use one until now. Micah came back to us and held us in his big arms.

I only knew Teddy as someone who saved creatures' lives, but here he was, the arbiter of death for a creature of God that held his heart. That Teddy knew what to do was a shock, and the fact that Teddy *could* do it changed him in my eyes. It seemed to me that a tenderhearted boy would have refused to take that necessary but unbearable step; I would have shared his pain. But it took a full-hearted man to see the creature he loved through death, to take that creature to the other side to ensure that it would not suffer as it found peace.

Teddy's commitment to that peace was so great that it steadied his hand, narrowed his grief, and brought calm to his every move. That calm in him calmed me. It was that calm in him that calmed Moss Star.

Moss Star seemed to sense the end. He reared his fearless head up, neighed one more time, but then became still. Teddy stood slightly off-center, aimed at the horse's forehead, and fired. Moss Star fell forward toward Teddy, but Teddy didn't flinch. He laid the shotgun on the ground, knelt down, and put his hand on Moss Star's neck. He nodded at Micah.

I don't know when I started crying, before or after Teddy fired. Micah wiped an arm across his eyes and held us while we wept. I had seen Mama wring the necks of a hundred chickens, but this was the first time I understood the power of killing. Something in me—and in Zora, too—fell and broke.

Teddy walked back to us dry-eyed, but I had never seen him look more sad.

Teddy spoke slowly and tenderly. "Sometimes death is the only way."

I wrapped my arms around him. I hugged him with no thought of ever letting him go. I wanted to take away from him a pain that must have been ten times my own. He hugged me back, resting his head against my forehead, while I wept for us both.

After a few minutes, Teddy gently pulled away from me, holding my face in his hands. He softly wiped my tears away with his thumbs.

To Teddy, Micah said, "You ready to go see Mr. Polk?"

Teddy nodded. Micah picked up the shotgun, put his arm around his younger brother, and the two of them walked toward Mr. Polk's place.

Zora and I made our way back to her house in

silence. I didn't trust my words not to come out in sobs. Tears still streamed from her eyes.

I hadn't felt this much pain since my father went missing. How could I have ever let foolish pride anger me toward Teddy? He was, like Eatonville itself, beautiful and kind and constant and true.

CHAPTER NINETEEN

The dim sunlight filtering through the low-hanging clouds cast long shadows. As we neared the Hurston property, those shadows stretched toward us like long, dark fingers. In them I saw shapes that made me shiver: the serpent-like coil of men's hate and the hard lines of the guns they expressed it with. Zora's shadow stretched backward toward the chicken yard and seemed to break apart. My own shadow dragged, unwilling to keep pace with my grief-filled heart.

On the porch we found Mrs. Hurston, her expression split between anger and relief. "Where have you two been? I should whip you myself!" Then relief seemed to win out over fear, and she pulled us to her. For a single second I couldn't think why she would be so worried about us on this day of all days. My grief over Moss Star and the tidal wave of feelings for Teddy had pushed everything else to the back of my mind. Now I was reminded of the threat to Eatonville.

I held on to Mrs. Hurston and Zora, our three shadows together forming a silty-gray carpet that spilled diagonally down the front steps of the house and out onto the path. It was that carpet that met Mr. Clarke and Mr. Cools as they rode up to the house, Mr. Clarke on his beautiful bay mare, Mr. Cools on his tall mule, each one carrying a shotgun, their faces masks of fierce resolution.

Mrs. Hurston stiffened. "Joe . . ." was all she managed to say.

Joe Clarke swung down, tied up his horse, and came over to us. He put his hand on Zora's shoulder and said, "We got word. They're riding tonight."

Mr. Cools called Mr. Hurston's name.

Mr. Hurston walked out onto the porch, shotgun in hand. He looked at his wife, his daughter, and me, and in his eyes I saw everything that ever made a man want to run. Then he looked at Joe Clarke. "They coming." It was a statement. Any questions of the previous night had been displaced by the certainty of impending bloodshed.

Joe Clarke nodded. "Eatonville has no borders tonight."

Lucy Hurston found her tongue, pushed us away, and moved to stand in front of her husband. She looked up into his face and warned, "You men stand against them and they come for all of us. They gonna come for all of us."

John Hurston put his hands on his wife's shoulders. At first I thought it was to steady her, but then I saw the truth. Lucy was his strength. He held her to draw that strength into his own body.

Zora's brother John came out of the house then, with Dick and Cliff close behind.

"Lucy, close the storm shutters, get inside, and lock the doors. No lamps." And without turning to his sons, Mr. Hurston added, "John, you come with me. Dick, Cliff, sit up with your guns at the ready." Dick and Cliff stood still as statues, the words knocking all the boyhood from their faces.

Within a minute, Mr. Clarke, Mr. Cools, Mr. Hurston, and John were all in the saddle and on the road.

As I followed the men in my mind, I realized that Teddy and Micah had unwittingly walked straight into the field of battle. Once they figured that out, there was no way they'd want to leave.

Half an hour later the only sounds in the living room were our breathing and the soft clip of scissors snipping thread. Mrs. Hurston and Sarah were working on quilt squares, a single lit candle between them. Cliff and Dick sat by the window, cradling their shotguns. This was the moment when our color became our curse—waiting to see if justice prevailed or if, like our men, we, too, would have to fight to the death. Feeling so helpless turned my fear to anger, anger so strong I thought I would explode.

I wasn't the only one feeling that way. Zora stood up. "Carrie and I are going to sit upstairs."

Mrs. Hurston just nodded as her fingers worked the needle in the flickering light. Sarah didn't look up, but she began to sniffle. Everett, sensing the tension in the room, began whimpering softly.

Mrs. Hurston pulled Everett onto her lap and said to Sarah, "Wipe your tears. The time to cry is after the worst is over. Now is the time to pray."

Zora and I climbed quietly upstairs and I lay down

on her bed. The cotton cover, slightly damp from the humid evening air, tickled my bare arms. Being scared and sad at the same time made my eyes burn, so I closed them tight.

Zora sat on Sarah's bed across the room.

"Well?" she asked. "What are you thinking?" I looked over to see her eyebrows arched and her mouth set in a firm line.

Zora responded to fear like a lion tamer in a ring. She would hold the beast away by sheer force of will. I pushed myself up on one elbow.

"I'm thinking that I'm glad my mama's away." I said it with all the conviction I could stir up, but in fact I was wishing with all my might that my mama were here with me. "I'm thinking," I said, "what if my mama comes home in two days and there ain't no home to come home to?"

Zora nodded. "If your mama heard even a hint of what's happening tonight, she'd ride the devil's own stallion to get to you."

I realized that if I talked the tears would come out, so I didn't say anything. I sat there, swallowing and feeling shame for wanting my mother with me more than I wanted her to be safely far away.

Zora came over next to me and put her arm

around my shoulders and hugged me to her. She wasn't Mama, but she was the next best thing. We stayed like that for a good little while, me not crying and Zora gently rubbing my arm, not saying a word, just letting me feel, and likely knowing that I had just told a lie.

Once the scared sadness inside me didn't feel so bottled up anymore, I could speak. "Your daddy and John and Micah and"—I paused and took a breath—"and Teddy are out there tonight."

My words hung in the sticky moist air. Zora pinched my arm—gently—and whispered, "Do you love Teddy?"

She knew. Of course she knew, but it wasn't her knowing the truth about my feelings that made them irrevocably real. It was her saying it out loud. It hit me that not telling her about Teddy was my way of not telling myself. Zora was my best self, my most truthful self, so her speaking those words aloud made them something I could never deny again. "Yes. I do. I love Teddy Baker."

Zora smiled. "I love you, Carrie Brown. I love Teddy Baker, too. I love you both like I love my own family."

Now it was my turn to hug her, and I did it with

all the strength I had. Hugging her gave me strength. "Zora, I think tonight's gonna decide the future of Eatonville. Our future. I want my mama to come home, and I want Teddy to be safe, but I know no amount of wishing is gonna make one or the other of those things happen."

She chewed her bottom lip. "I can't hardly sit here another minute while half the folks we love in the world are out there facing down death."

"I know!" I agreed wholeheartedly. "Let's go!"

Zora squinted at me. "Really? You want to go? I don't have to convince you?"

"Yes, I want to go! Right now! But how do we get out of here?"

Zora put her finger to her lips. She slid the window up slowly and quietly with the skill of a seasoned burglar. "We climb."

I had climbed up so many trees and vines that climbing held no special fear for me. But we weren't climbing up—we were climbing down, like Orpheus deliberately descending to Hades. And Hades is where we were headed, as sure as the sun breaks dawn in the east.

I climbed out onto the warm roof over the kitchen

side of the house, slid over to the drainpipe, and eased myself down it, cat-quiet.

Zora was by my side a minute later, and we were over the fence and off down the road, careful to stay to the side so we could jump into the grass and hide if anyone approached.

CHAPTER TWENTY

When we reached the pasture at the western edge of Mr. Polk's property, most of the men who had been in the Hurston living room were there, along with a few others who hadn't — like Teddy and Micah. All were facing away from us, turned in the direction of the road that led to Lake Maitland. Besides Mr. Polk himself, Teddy was the only one not holding a gun.

Zora put her hand on my arm and pointed at Mr. Polk's stables, which stood between us and the men. Ducking low, we made our way to the stables and hid ourselves in the stall that had belonged until that afternoon to Moss Star, the worn slats leaving enough space for peeking. Through the clouds we could see the last dark-red of the sun sinking slowly over the horizon, light giving way to this terrible night.

The men of Eatonville did not grow darker with the fading light; rather, they seemed to shine brighter in it. The darker-hued ones glowed incandescent, as if the moon were illuminating them from within. The lighter-skinned ones appeared coral, like the husk of the cactus flower.

These men had fathered and made this town whole in spite of the hate of an entire nation. These men had picked cotton, oranges, and tobacco from sunup to sundown and still came home most days shunning misery and weaving wonder with tales about outsmarting Ole Massa and the devil, too. These men made women laugh at least as much as they made them cry, and they preached sermons so we had a code for living, built houses so we had a place to live, and dug graves so we had a place to rest when we died.

These men refused to be hardened by the yoke or the whip of white men or by fear. Instead of being immobilized by their own degradation, they became brave beyond measure.

These men had come from places that said our town was something only a fool would dream, then dreamed Eatonville into existence. They then swore a blood oath to protect it with their lives. To take some was to take all. Each man here was ready to hold everything he loved up against the price of losing one square inch of Eatonville. Eatonville represented freedom itself.

Those men, so much like my father, held all my hope. If they fell, we fell; if they stood, we could stand. They had as much hope of standing past morning as the cactus flower itself. And yet here they stood.

Hoofbeats sounded in the distance, and the men took their places outside Mr. Polk's cabin. Mr. Polk, Mr. Clarke, and Mr. Hurston stood at the front. I squeezed Zora's wrist so hard she had to pry open my fingers and take my hand.

It was a lone rider, and as he came close we could see it was Mr. Ambrose, with a rifle scabbard slung across his back. He dismounted, and the first thing he did was clasp Mr. Polk's hand in both of his. We couldn't hear what he said to Mr. Polk, but when he stepped back he addressed the group clearly.

"Gentlemen, I got word of trouble that might be

coming your way. I went to the Lake Maitland sheriff to see if he could help, but he wasn't interested, I'm sorry to say. But I'm here to stand with you tonight. If necessary, I'm here to put my gun with yours. The threat to you is a threat to what I know is right."

Joe Clarke stepped forward and shook hands with Mr. Ambrose, and Mr. Hurston and Doc Brazzle did the same. Mr. Polk tethered Mr. Ambrose's horse to the fence, and then they waited. We waited.

Everyone's ears locked onto the slightest sound. Zora and I didn't dare speak a word. Sweat trickled down my armpits, and ghost ants crawled across my feet.

About half an hour later hoofbeats broke the silence again, this time much louder, meaning plenty of riders. It was the two white men from Joe Clarke's store plus five other white men, all on horseback, all armed, two carrying torches. I had half expected them to be wearing disguises; I had once overheard Mrs. Sinkler tell my mama they did that in Jacksonville. "Too ashamed to show their devil faces, I suspect," Mrs. Sinkler had said. "They ride all twisted up in white sheets, like the evil spirits they are." But these men had no shame. They were boldly themselves. The two we had seen at Joe Clarke's store were in frock coats, two others were in shirtsleeves, two in bib overalls, and one still in butcher whites. I recognized the last of them as Mr. Carter, and the shock of it made my stomach twist. That a man I knew, and who knew me and my mama by name, could set out to hurt the people I loved most in the world because another white man wanted land that belonged to a black man. No matter how long I lived, the hate white folks could have toward us would never make sense to me.

The white-haired man pulled his horse to a halt in front of Joe Clarke and Mr. Polk.

Joe Clarke stepped forward and addressed him. "Mr. Peterson, we don't want no trouble."

But this Mr. Peterson had already dismounted, pointedly ignoring Mr. Clarke, and addressed the other Eatonville men in Polk's yard. "This ain't your quarrel, boys," he said. "Go home to your wives and children. Leave Horatio Polk and me to talk this out, and nothing will happen to you and yours. You have my word."

Not a single man moved.

"This is a private matter between two men," Mr. Peterson asserted. "It needs to be settled privately."

Mr. Slayton pointed to the bruise on the side of Mr. Peterson's face. "Looks like you tried that already. Looks like it ain't been settled, leastways not the way you wanted it to be."

Mr. Peterson's tone shot from reason to rage in a flash. "This is my land!" His anger was like a signal to the men who had ridden with him to raise their guns. But in the next moment, the circle of Eatonville men tightened, and the white men found themselves outnumbered three to one and looking down the barrels of nineteen rifles and shotguns. Still, the white men sat easy on their horses, comfortable even.

A slow, sad awareness began to dawn on me. It didn't matter how many guns we had. Their whiteness was stronger than our guns. Their skin itself was their power. Even if we shot them dead, the power of their whiteness would live on to see us all hanged. Our men were not real to them; they were mere shadows, without substance or soul.

My throat burned and my eyes stung. Our lives mattered just as much as theirs, but the truth of that had been erased by slavery. Slavery itself might be over, but neither the Thirteenth Amendment nor anything that had happened since could make us human in the eyes of these men. That was why our parents had fought so hard to create and sustain a corner of the world where we determined our own value.

Mr. Clarke slowly set his rifle on the ground. "Lower your weapons, men," he said, letting his own hands float down deliberately, as if he were God nudging clouds from Heaven toward Earth. "Lower your weapons."

Not until they saw the Eatonville men ease their grips and lower their weapons did the white men do the same, slowly. This made Mr. Peterson angrier. "It *is* my land, by God. It is my legacy."

Mr. Clarke nodded and said, "I know you think so, Mr. Peterson, but the law says differently." He held up his left hand in a gesture of surrender while reaching into a pocket with his right. He carefully pulled out a piece of paper, unfolded it, and held it out. "This here is the deed to this land, and it belongs to Horatio Polk, who bought it from me outright for cash. The law says this land was mine to sell to him when the town of Eatonville was founded in 1887."

"*Your* deed means nothing against a white man's rights!" Mr. Peterson was shouting now.

"Is that so, Timothy?" It was the voice of Old Lady Bronson. She stepped out onto the porch from inside Mr. Polk's cabin. Her silver hair, loose for only the second time I'd seen it in all the years I had known her, was a glowing halo against the night sky. Tiny as she was, I could feel the air electrify with her presence.

She stepped off the porch and walked over to Mr. Peterson until she stood a nose away from him. "Timothy," she said, "it took you decades to come back. Did you think I must be gone, or did you forget about me altogether? Or maybe you thought I would have forgotten?"

Mr. Peterson was blinking hard, like he was trying to clear his vision, and his mouth was open but no sound was coming out.

Mr. Ambrose, who had been standing in shadow at the back of the group, came forward and stood next to Old Lady Bronson. Seeing him, the other white men exchanged wary glances. "I'm surprised, too, Timothy," said Mr. Ambrose. "I would have thought this would be the last place you'd ever dare to come back to."

"Lucia," Mr. Peterson croaked. "Jude." The fire fueling his rage seemed to be extinguished all at once.

One of Peterson's posse frowned and, gesturing toward Mr. Ambrose, asked, "Mr. Peterson, do you know this man?"

Not waiting for Mr. Peterson himself to answer, Mr. Ambrose scoffed. "Know us? He's the architect of our lives." As he spoke, Mr. Ambrose casually reached behind his back and drew out his rifle, careful to hold it barrel-down. Then he turned to the riders and named them. "Jeffrey, Tulane, Bobby, Matthew, Macon. I suspect you don't know this man at all. I'm guessing he paid you some money, gave you some whiskey, and promised you a good time stringing up an uppity colored man. But if you've come for Horatio, you're going to have to shoot me, too. Are you sure you want to shoot me along with your colored neighbors? Are you sure you want to do that—for a stranger?"

The white men began shifting in their saddles. The hateful confidence they had come with appeared to be splintering. The one called Tulane spoke like a whiny child. "Jude, we ain't white men no more if nigras can go ahead and buy and sell the land our fathers died for."

"Our fathers, our uncles, our brothers, and our friends died for a lot of reasons," Mr. Ambrose intoned slowly, "but none of them likely died to defend this murderer." I don't know whether or not they had been drinking, but the words of Mr. Ambrose certainly seemed to sober them. At the word *murderer*, all the men, white *and* colored, looked confused.

The land developer, looking from his client to Mr. Ambrose, seemed uncertain. "What are you talking about? And whether or not these people are familiar with my client doesn't alter his legitimate claim to this land!"

Mr. Ambrose looked the land developer right in the eye and spoke in a steely voice. "In 1855, Timothy Peterson, the man you represent and whom the rest of you have decided to ride with, killed the woman I was going to marry, the woman who today should be my wife. I know this because Horatio Polk and Lucia Bronson were there. They saw him kill her then, which is why he wants nothing more than for you to kill Horatio now; he wants you to do his dirty work. That's what kind of a liar and a coward he is."

The men Mr. Peterson had gathered from Lake Maitland leaned forward in their saddles and whispered to one another. Mr. Peterson looked huffy and irritated. It was clear to us that he couldn't hear what they were whispering, and that it was no accident.

"Tulane," called Mr. Ambrose, "let me make this simple for you. If you choose to take the law into your own hands using the noose you've got tied to your saddle, I'll choose to take the law into mine." He raised the polished barrel of his rifle and pointed it straight at Timothy Peterson's chest. "And my justice has been waiting a long, long time."

Mr. Peterson caught his breath but didn't say a word. Not one of the men who had come with him raised a finger or a voice to defend him.

The one called Tulane shook his head. "I don't know what-all you done, Peterson, and I don't much care, but you never said we'd be facing down Jude Ambrose and a couple dozen coloreds with shotguns. And you don't got to do business with Jude, but I do. We all do." He looked at the other men on horseback, and they all nodded in agreement.

Old Lady Bronson nudged the muzzle of Mr. Ambrose's rifle away from Peterson and toward the ground. "Timothy," she proclaimed, "I don't need a gun to face you down."

Peterson reached up as if to push her away from him, but she, the quicker one, slapped his hand down. The land developer let out a startled cry.

Old Lady Bronson's laughter carried like the sound of a fast train. "You can't escape your ghosts, Timothy." Even from where we were hiding, I could see he was trembling. "Sooner or later they find you. It took almost half a century, but here you are. And you probably thought the choice to return was yours, didn't you?" She shook her head, as if amazed by his stupidity. "I cursed you all those years ago. I cursed you and this land. Look around!" She gestured toward the fallow expanse of Mr. Polk's property. "My curse isn't even close to being finished. You've come back for nothing and you will leave with nothing. You'll leave with less than you came with. I don't care how far you run, Timothy. The justice behind my words will always find you." And with that she spat at his feet. Every man there recoiled with fear; even white folks gave wide berth to the mysterious reach of hoodoo.

Peterson turned away from her fierce stare, turned to the men he came with, and for a minute struggled to speak. "Don't you see?" he finally sputtered. "She knows the land is mine. Her and Horatio, they want to cheat me. She'll do anything to cheat me. She hates me. She wants you to hate me." He backed away from Old Lady Bronson, almost stumbling before grabbing the reins of his horse.

Old Lady Bronson stepped toward him again.

"You think hate will rule this day the way it ruled that night forty-eight years ago. You think hate is why

I cursed you. You think hate is what I've been nursing in my bosom all these years, like the venom you've been nursing in yours. I did hate you, Timothy, but those were the feelings of a grieving girl. Since then I've traveled beyond hate, far beyond it, all the way to justice. Justice and hate can't sit at the same table, so do not leave here in the smug certainty that I hate you. Hating you would make a mockery of my love — for my sister, for my people, for myself. No, Timothy. Leave here knowing that justice found you. That your crimes have been witnessed."

Mr. Peterson seemed to crumple in on himself. He gathered the reins of his horse and retreated up into his saddle. From there he should have towered over Old Lady Bronson, but he only looked shrunken and small. "Shoot her!" he commanded to the men he'd duped into following him, but not a one moved. Any power he might have had turned counterfeit. Faced with mutiny, he kicked his horse in the ribs and fled back down the road toward Lake Maitland.

Old Lady Bronson looked at the land developer, who'd also climbed back into his saddle. "Tell me, boy." Her voice was loud and clear as a bell. "Do you think this land is worth the price you'd have to pay to get it?" She was not asking a question. Rather, she was making a declaration of war.

The white man, overcome by Old Lady Bronson's fierceness, offered no response. Avoiding all eyes, he turned his horse away and rode after Mr. Peterson.

Now leaderless, the men remaining murmured among themselves. Zora and I couldn't make out a word from where we sat. Finally, the one called Tulane addressed Mr. Ambrose.

"You've known us all our lives, Jude. We was just out for a bit of fun. For sure, no harm was done tonight, so no need to speak on this again." The others nodded their quick assent. Such was the ease with which they could choose to take life and then choose not to.

Those men rode away at a leisurely pace, as if they were returning home after a picnic. We watched the light of their torches shrink to dots and then disappear.

Every man's eyes turned now to Old Lady Bronson, but no one seemed to know what to do or say next. It was she who broke the spell by placing her hand gently on Mr. Ambrose's rifle arm. Before our very eyes, Mr. Ambrose collapsed like a hollowed-out shell. He took her slender hand in his large ones, and said, "Thank you, Lucia."

She nodded and said, "Good-bye, Jude."

Mr. Ambrose sheathed his rifle, untied his horse, and rode slowly away, his back a little bowed.

Now that all the white men were gone, the Eatonville men finally put up their guns. A few exchanged hugs, like brothers might. Mr. Clarke shook Old Lady Bronson's hand like she was a visiting dignitary. Then, one after the other, the rest of the men did the same, right down to Teddy. After all the years I'd spent being scared at the mere mention of her name, I now found myself bursting with pride to know Old Lady Bronson. Zora took my hand and pumped it up and down in exaggerated imitation of the men.

Mr. Baker, Teddy, Micah, and Jake walked off toward their farm. With the threat gone and Teddy safe, the knot in my belly, tight as a fist, began to loosen.

Mr. Hurston, John, Mr. Clarke, and Old Lady Bronson walked Mr. Polk to his door. Once he was safely inside, Mr. Clarke and Mr. Hurston offered to walk Old Lady Bronson home. She thanked them but shook her head. "I've got some unfinished business" was all she said. They deferred to her will and then turned westward toward the heart of Eatonville.

CHAPTER TWENTY-ONE

Z ora and I finally dared to stand and took in a deep breath of the air of the town that still belonged to us.

A soft chuckle spun us around. In the doorway of our stall stood Old Lady Bronson. She cocked her head at us, like a bird of prey. "Well, I reckon you girls can come with me, now." It seemed her *unfinished business* was us!

We followed her dutifully but didn't utter a word. Were we about to get a lecture? A scolding? Was she, personally, returning us to Zora's parents?

The home she led us to was her own. She opened
the door and we followed her in, half expecting to be
led to a dungeon. Then she began lighting kerosene
lamps. We were stunned. Inside, the cottage looked
much larger than it did from the outside. Every wall,
from floor to ceiling, was whitewashed and lined with
books. Some of the bindings were worn, the leather
tattered, and the color long faded like flags left out
in the sun. Others were being held together by a thin
cord or twine. The furniture was equally surprising:
a table was covered in cloth the color of blue sky
with jewel-toned flower-shaped patches sewn onto it;
the backs of her wooden chairs were carved with the
shapes of birds, work I recognized as that of our old
neighbor Mr. Pendir. And in one corner of the room
stood a wingback chair covered in crimson leather.
The seat had worn down to muted brown, but the
headrest glistened as if it had been oiled only yesterday. It was a throne, not of some flamboyant queen
but of a monarch steeped in the study of life.

Zora walked slowly, reverently, to the nearest shelf
of books. "These books aren't in English," she breathed,
running her hand across their leather bindings.

Old Lady Bronson watched us, a satisfied glint in

her eye. "They are in Spanish and French. The languages I grew up with."

"Which one did you talk to Mr. Polk in?" Zora asked, her hand still caressing the books.

"Spanish," said Old Lady Bronson with a small smile.

"Spanish." Zora repeated the word as if it were an enchantment.

In my politest voice, I asked, "Miz Bronson, where are you from?" That evening, my childhood fear of her had been replaced by awe. She might be a witch, but she was also a woman who stood up to a lynch mob. The strongest magic she possessed was courage, and I longed for some of it to rub off on me.

"I was born on the island of Hispaniola. Like America, it was a slave country, but years before I was born, the slaves fought for their freedom and won. Half my island would reject that freedom, but Haiti, the land where my mother was born, has stayed free to this day." She walked over to a round globe, so old some of the leather across the Atlantic Ocean had worn away. She turned it and pointed to a spot below what we knew to be Florida. "That was my first home. The place where I was born."

Zora put her finger on the spot tenderly, the way you might caress a sleeping infant's face. "Hispaniola," she said quietly, more to herself than to us. "I would like to see Hispaniola."

Old Lady Bronson leaned in close to Zora and lowered her voice. "If you really do, then keep your shoes pointing south while you sleep. On Sunday, light a candle next to a blue heron feather in the southeast corner of your bedroom. You'll see Hispaniola, Zora Neale. That I can promise you."

Zora's face was aglow. Right here in front of us was the biggest mystery in all of Eatonville: a woman who straddled two countries, three languages, and worlds seen and unseen.

"Miz Bronson—" Zora began.

Old Lady Bronson interrupted. "I think you two have earned the right to call me Miz Lucia."

"Miz Lucia," Zora said shyly. Her voice softened as she asked the next question. "Who was the woman Timothy Peterson killed?"

Miz Lucia sank into the red leather armchair, motioning us to sit before her.

"My sister."

Nothing she said could have shocked me more.

"But Mr. Ambrose said he was going to marry her."

"He was. That's true."

"But, then, your sister would have to be white."

"She was."

"Your sister was white?" Zora put words to my disbelief.

"Yes. We had the same father," she gently explained. "It was a secret we didn't discover until I was fourteen years old."

Zora pressed further. "Why would Mr. Peterson shoot her, Miz Lucia?"

"He shot her because she was trying to escape north with me."

She reached over and took a small, round framed photograph from the table next to her chair. "This was Prisca."

Zora took it and we stared at it hard. "You have the same eyes," Zora said.

Miz Lucia nodded.

I took the photograph so I could peer at it more closely. I trembled. "She's dressed just like the lady in the woods!"

Miz Lucia looked at me sharply. "You've seen her?"

Zora looked surprised, too.

Taking turns, Zora and I told Old Lady Bronson

everything about our trip to the old plantation and the strange sounds and sights we had seen by the pond.

Miz Lucia sat back, quiet and watchful, for several long moments.

"I still owe you a story, Zora, but today you have earned more than that. You've earned the truth that I kept from you two nights ago." She took a deep breath. "I can remember the sharp taste of salt in the air. We stood in front of the ship at dawn, the day already hot. . . ."

For the next half hour she told us the story of how she was born free and became a slave. What she described was cruel beyond anything I had imagined and soaked me in sorrow. It was clear to me now why the men in the Hurston living room would so willingly risk their lives to protect Eatonville. Freedom was life; slavery was a living death. Miz Lucia had known both in one lifetime. Even as night riders and hatred could still snatch our safety away, Zora and I, by the grace of forty years, had only known lives as free people.

"Why didn't you move away from here?" I demanded. "Why would you stay in a place with such painful memories?"

"Because everyone I love is of this land. Because

of Horatio, because of the community that grew up around me, and because of Prisca's memory. I gave my own daughters wings and watched them perch both near and far. But I stay because no one will ever have the power to make me leave a place ever again."

"And Mr. Polk?"

"Horatio and I became kin on this land. And when it came up for sale, he bought it. It was the only other time I heard him speak in the past fifty years." There were tears in her eyes as she said this.

I recalled the way Mr. Polk had looked at Old Lady Bronson the night he was stabbed. He loved her the way I loved Zora. He would do anything for her. The family you're born to is your lifeblood, but the family you choose is your heart.

By looking only at the outside of the lives of Miz Lucia and Mr. Polk, I had failed to truly see them at all. I had mistaken Mr. Polk's silence for muteness and Old Lady Bronson's strength for malevolence.

"Timothy Peterson changed a lot of lives the night he killed my sister," she continued. "All our lives altered because a boy wanted to prove to his father that he was man enough to own other human beings." She shook her head. "Slavery is over, but tonight you saw how it still haunts us."

I spoke up now. "I understand the how, but I still don't understand the why." Then I asked the question I had been burning to ask my whole life. "Why do they hate us so much?"

Old Lady Bronson reached down and took my chin in her hand, firmly yet gently. "They have to hate because you can't take another person's freedom with love."

It was a simple answer, yet contained a universe of truth.

Zora still had a million questions, so Miz Lucia brewed a sweet pot of hot lemon with mint and poured us cup after cup through Zora's many questions. Miz Lucia gave generous helpings of answers, and we listened like devoted students. It was the first time we would sit at her knee like this, but it would not be the last. For Zora it would mark an awakening to learning, a lifelong striving to understand the world beyond our town and our ways.

For me, it was an awakening to who I was, to who we were, and a new understanding of where we came from and what we, as a people, had endured. As I realized how close to slavery we still were, Eatonville meant more to me than ever. And I marveled all the more at Joe Clarke and the men and women of

Eatonville, at their courage and vision in creating a town so dedicated to our freedom.

When Zora and I finally left Miz Lucia's bungalow, the storm clouds of the previous two days were blowing gently to the south, revealing a pale moon hanging low against a clear inky sky.

"My daddy's going to tan our hides clear to Sunday," Zora said.

"I know," I said with an unfamiliar calm.

"There's still something I have to ask you. How come you didn't tell me you saw a woman by the horse?"

"I don't know," I answered truthfully. "That day was full of so many confusing things. I just assumed you had seen her, too. Then I thought maybe I had imagined her, that maybe I had scared myself into seeing a ghost."

"What do you think now?"

"Now I think I must have been seeing a memory so powerful it could come alive for a moment."

"So how come we both saw the horse, but only you saw the woman?"

"I—I didn't see the horse. I just saw the woman. You saw the horse, but not the woman."

Zora stopped walking and turned to look at me. "We each saw a different piece of the same memory," she breathed. "Here we are, thinking we're each living our own lives, but maybe we're all just pieces of a bigger puzzle. Maybe we're part of some other people's memory right now, creating the story of people we haven't even met."

I smiled. Zora's mind was already busy turning the last two days into a story, one that would become richer and richer with each telling—our history in beautiful, polished words.

We walked on, our bare feet leaving small dusty prints in the sandy Florida dirt. The storm having passed over us, those tracks would just as surely be there in the morning as we would be off somewhere else, living the next bit of our lives. However much we were each other's future, we were irrevocably one another's past.

ZORA NEALE HURSTON

A Biography

To hear Zora Neale Hurston tell it, she was born in Eatonville, Florida, the daughter of a mayor, in 1901, or 1903, or 1910. Even from a young age, Hurston was an inventor of stories, a creator of masks and disguises. In reality, she was born in 1891 in Notasulga, Alabama, the fifth of eight children raised by John and Lucy Hurston. Her mother was a schoolteacher and her father, born into slavery, a carpenter and preacher (who did eventually become the mayor of Eatonville).

Although Alabama was her place of birth, Eatonville, Florida, was the place that truly felt like home to Zora. It was the first incorporated all-black township in the United States, established by twenty-seven African-American men soon after the Emancipation Proclamation. Hurston and her family moved to Eatonville when she was just a toddler, and the thriving community infected her with energy, confidence, and ambition. Hurston's childhood was idyllic.

But then in 1904, when Hurston was just thirteen, her mother passed away. Thus began what Zora would later call the "haunted years." Lucy Hurston had been the one to encourage her daughter to have courageous dreams. John Hurston encouraged his daughter, too, but just as often tried to tame her rambunctious spirit, sometimes harshly. After his wife died, John had little energy or money to devote to his children and grew detached from them emotionally. When he remarried, his new wife and Zora were like oil and water.

Zora left home after a vicious fight with the new Mrs. Hurston and struggled to finish high school while working a variety of different jobs. One of those jobs was working as a maid to a singer in a traveling theater troupe, an experience that sparked Hurston's love of performance, a passion that would last the rest of her life. In 1917, she found herself in Baltimore. She was twenty-six and still without her high-school diploma. So Hurston lied about her age, convincing the school that she was sixteen so that she could re-enroll and complete her education. From that point on, Hurston would always present herself as younger than she actually was.

In 1919, Hurston entered college, first at Howard University and then at Barnard College, where she was the only black student and studied under the famous anthropologist Franz Boas. During these years, her writing began to get recognized. Her first short story, "John Redding Goes to Sea," was published in Howard University's literary magazine in 1921.

In the 1920s, Hurston moved to New York City and became an integral part of the Harlem Renaissance, befriending poet Langston Hughes and singer-actress Ethel Waters, among many other cultural luminaries. Zora was the life of the party, frequently hosting artists at her home (though she retreated into her room when she needed to get any writing done).

In 1933, publisher Bertram Lippincott read Hurston's short story "The Gilded Six-Bits" and inquired as to whether she might be working on a novel. Hurston answered yes — and then set to work writing one, which became *Jonah's Gourd Vine*. By 1935, Hurston had her first novel and a collection of southern folktales under her publishing belt.

In 1936, the travel dust that Hurston's mother thought must have been sprinkled in her shoes allowed her to leave the shores of North America. After applying for and receiving a Guggenheim Fellowship, she traveled to Haiti on the island of Hispaniola and to Jamaica to study indigenous religious practices. In both places, she was a keen observer as well as a full participant in *vodoun* practices.

In 1937, Hurston's most renowned novel, *Their Eyes Were Watching God*, was published. In that novel, Hurston's heroine, Janie Crawford, lives a conventionally circumscribed life until she chooses to break out of the mold and live only for herself. Much like Hurston, Janie has her eyes on the horizon and believes in a better life beyond it. The novel has been praised as a classic of black literature and a tribute to the strength of black women.

Hurston went on to write several other works, including a study of Caribbean voodoo practices, two more novels, and her autobiography, *Dust Tracks on a Road*. All in all, she wrote four novels and more than fifty short stories, plays, and essays. Sadly, Hurston never enjoyed any monetary reward for her success during her lifetime. When she died in 1960 at the age of sixty-nine, her neighbors had to take up a collection for the funeral. Hurston was buried in an unmarked grave in Fort Pierce, Florida, because the neighbors hadn't been able to raise enough funds for a funeral *and* a gravestone.

In 1973, a young writer named Alice Walker traveled to Fort Pierce to visit the burial site of the woman who had inspired so many black female authors with her courage and strength: Hurston had insisted on living life on her own terms during a time when most women, and especially black women, had few professional options. "A people do not forget their geniuses," Walker said, and arranged to have a monument placed, at last, to honor the life and achievements of Zora Neale Hurston.

A Time Line of Zora Neale Hurston's Life

1891
Born in Notasulga, Alabama, the fifth of eight children, to John Hurston, a carpenter and preacher, and Lucy Potts Hurston, a former schoolteacher.

1894
The Hurston family moves to Eatonville, Florida, a small all-black community.

1897
Hurston's father is elected mayor of Eatonville.

1904
Lucy Potts Hurston dies.

1917–1918
Attends Morgan Academy in Baltimore, Maryland, and completes high-school requirements.

1918
Works as a waitress at a nightclub and a manicurist at a barbershop that serves only whites.

1919–1924
Attends Howard University and receives an associate degree.

1921
Publishes her first story, "John Redding Goes to Sea," in Howard University's literary magazine.

1925–1927
Moves to New York City and attends Barnard College as its only black student. Receives a bachelor of arts degree.

1927
Goes to Florida to collect folktales.

1927
Marries Herbert Sheen.

1930–1932
Organizes the field notes that become *Mules and Men.*

1930
Works on the play *Mule Bone* with Langston Hughes.

1931
Breaks with Langston Hughes over the authorship of *Mule Bone.*

1931
Divorces Sheen.

1934
Publishes *Jonah's Gourd Vine,* her first novel.

1935
Mules and Men, a collection of folklore, is published.

1936
Awarded a Guggenheim Fellowship to study West Indian *obeah* practices. Travels to Jamaica and Haiti. While in Haiti, she writes *Their Eyes Were Watching God* in seven weeks.

1937
Their Eyes Were Watching God is published.

1938
Tell My Horse is published.

1939
Receives an honorary doctor of letters degree from Morgan State College.

1939
Marries Albert Price III. They are later divorced.

1939
Moses, Man of the Mountain is published.

1942
Hurston's autobiography, *Dust Tracks on a Road,* is published.

1947
Goes to British Honduras to research black communities and writes *Seraph on the Suwanee.*

1948
Seraph on the Suwanee is published.

1956
Works as a librarian at Patrick Air Force Base, Florida.

1958
Works as a substitute teacher at Lincoln Park Academy in Fort Pierce, Florida.

1959
Suffers a stroke and enters the St. Lucie County Welfare Home.

1960
Dies in the St. Lucie County Welfare Home. Buried in an unmarked grave in Fort Pierce.

ZORA NEALE HURSTON

An Annotated Bibliography

The Complete Stories (1995)

Published after her death, this collection features Zora Neale Hurston's short fiction, which was originally published in literary magazines during her lifetime. Spanning Hurston's writing career from 1921 to 1955, the compilation showcases the writer's range, rich language, and development as a storyteller.

Dust Tracks on a Road (1942)

Hurston's autobiography tells the story of her rise from poverty to literary prominence. The writer's story is told with imagination and exuberance and offers a glimpse into the life of one of America's most esteemed writers.

Every Tongue Got to Confess: Negro Folk-Tales from the Gulf States (2001)

Originally collected by Hurston in 1927, this volume of folklore passed down through generations offers a glimpse of the African-American experience in the South at the turn of the century.

Jonah's Gourd Vine (1934)
Hurston's first published novel. Based loosely on her parents' lives, it features a preacher and his wife as the main characters.

Moses, Man of the Mountain (1939)
An allegory based on the story of the Exodus and blending the Moses of the Old Testament with the Moses of black folklore and song. Narrated in a mixture of biblical rhetoric, black dialect, and colloquial English.

Mule Bone: A Comedy of Negro Life (1930)
A collaboration between Hurston and Langston Hughes, this comedic play is set in Eatonville, Florida, and focuses on the lives of two men and the woman who comes between them. Due to a copyright disagreement between Hurston and Hughes, the play was not performed until 1991.

Mules and Men (1935)
Gathered by Hurston in the 1930s, the first great

collection of black America's folk world, including oral histories, sermons, and songs, some dating as far back as the Civil War.

Seraph on the Suwanee (1948)
A novel that explores the nature of love, faith, and marriage set at the turn of the century among white "Florida Crackers."

Tell My Horse: Voodoo and Life in Haiti and Jamaica (1938)
Hurston's travelogue of her time spent in Haiti and Jamaica in the 1930s practicing and learning about voodoo ceremonies, customs, and superstitions.

Their Eyes Were Watching God (1937)
The most widely read and highly acclaimed novel in African-American literature and the piece of writing for which Zora Neale Hurston is best known. Tells the story of Janie Crawford as she develops a sense of self through three marriages and grows into an independent woman.

Children's Books Adapted from
Folktales Collected by Zora Neale Hurston

———•———

Lies and Other Tall Tales. Adapted and illustrated by Christopher Myers. New York: HarperCollins, 2005.

The Six Fools. Adapted by Joyce Carol Thomas. Illustrated by Ann Tanksley. New York: HarperCollins, 2005.

The Skull Talks Back and Other Haunting Tales. Adapted by Joyce Carol Thomas. Illustrated by Leonard Jenkins. New York: HarperCollins, 2004.

The Three Witches. Adapted by Joyce Carol Thomas. Illustrated by Faith Ringgold. New York: HarperCollins, 2006.

What's the Hurry, Fox? and Other Animal Stories. Adapted by Joyce Carol Thomas. Illustrated by Bryan Collier. New York: HarperCollins, 2004.

ACKNOWLEDGMENTS

This book owes its deepest debt to my husband, Richard Simon, who reads and edits my work, nurturing and supporting it—and our family—every day. My life would be impoverished and my creative work impossible without him. I also owe a tremendous debt to my loved ones and early readers Viviana Simon, Hildegard McKinnon, Ayana Byrd, Abouali Farmanfarmaian, Rishi Gandhi, Dionne Bennett, and Nan Mooney; to Victoria Bond, cocreator of the first of these books, whose poetic voice was the key to finding *Zora and Me*; to Zora's niece, Lucy Hurston, for reading the final draft and giving the book her warm praise and blessing; and to my tireless agent, Victoria Sanders. Gratitude and affection go to my editors Mary Lee Donovan, who has championed *Zora and Me* from the beginning and whose patience, eagle eye, and gifted editorial pen helped me hew closer to my vision, and Andrea Tompa, who carefully sorted wheat from chaff and lovingly held my hand by e-mail for months, and to the whole talented and supportive Candlewick family. Finally, my lifelong gratitude belongs to Zora Neale Hurston, whose life and legacy continue to be a beacon for so many of us who seek to bring the stories of beautiful everyday black life to the center of our cultural narrative.